Maybe Baby
Texas Hardts

E.E. BURKE

Cover Design by Original Syn
Photography by Rob Lang
Formatting by Author E.M.S.

Published by E.E. Burke
978-0-9980712-4-4

*For my sweet Freckles
whose goal in life is to be happy...
and chase squirrels.*

Chapter One

May 18, 2015
Druid Hills, Northeast Atlanta

*A*long the tree-lined sidewalk, a woman in running gear kept pace with a towheaded little boy, wobbling on what looked like his first bike. Jen slowed her car, just in case the child lost control and weaved into the street. He didn't even look at her as he crossed the entrance to her driveway, peddling for all he was worth. His mother gave a wave as she passed.

Jen watched them wistfully for another moment before she pulled in. Lately, her nesting instincts had kicked in big time. The urgent *tick, tick* she kept hearing wasn't coming from her smart watch. She'd passed thirty, still unmarried, and based on her track record, had a high probability of remaining single. If she wanted to have a child, she'd better do it now, and on her own—as she'd done just about everything else in her life.

She hurried into the house, changed into her workout clothes and let the dog into the back yard. Why not practice yoga on the brick patio and enjoy the pleasant fall weather?

Afterwards, after she got done with her calls, she could do more research and, with luck, find a potential sperm donor. That way, she could get what she wanted, while avoiding uncomfortable entanglements.

With a deep breath, she lifted her arms to the sun, and then bent, planting her palms on the mat and pushing her hips toward the sky, stepping back with each foot until her body formed an inverted V. A spotted muzzle nudged aside her dangling ponytail and sniffed.

"Go on, silly. We'll play later."

Freckles dashed off, no doubt to chase one of the many squirrels up one of the many pine trees or into the branches of a hundred-year-old live oak. The dog couldn't roam far. High hedges concealed a wrought iron fence enclosing the yard, extra security for pets...and children.

Exhaling, Jen gazed upside down between her legs at the rear of a renovated Tudor that looked like a transplant from Stratford-upon-Avon. The dense shrubs and leafy canopy reminded her of the secret garden out of a book she'd escaped into as a child. Her dog wasn't the only one who favored the new digs over their last home, a one-bedroom apartment in Manhattan. What a relief to inhale fresh air that smelled of grass, not garbage. She'd made the right decision to take over the agency's Atlanta office and move into an historic neighborhood close to her job downtown, yet with a low crime rate and top-notch schools, the perfect place to raise a family.

The challenge now would be to find the perfect donor. She distrusted sperm banks. After all, she wouldn't purchase a car without driving it, or a house without walking through it, or even fresh produce without having a chance to touch it. No, that wasn't a good analogy. She had a lengthy list of requirements, but touching wasn't one of them.

A number of business associates were bright, successful men, reasonably good-looking and seemingly healthy; one of them might donate. Except, seeing the donor on a regular basis would make business meetings awkward.

Ideally, he would be someone she could meet, investigate thoroughly, but have no ties to him. How could she go about finding this Mr. Right? Rather, *Mr. Y*, who could provide the chromosome she needed, as well as impressive DNA.

A throat-clearing sound came from behind.

Jen snapped her eyes open, her head still down, and looked out between her legs. She stared in confusion at scuffed cowboy boots, topped by worn jeans, covering manly legs that seemed to go on forever.

With a gasp, she leapt out of the pose and spun around; bad enough to be caught off guard by a total stranger, much less with her ass in the air. Instinctively, she assumed a defensive stance, and looked up...and up... At five-six, she wasn't considered short, but the intruder had to be well over six feet. She was forced to tilt her head to look him in the eye. Her tongue cleaved to the roof of her mouth.

The color of his eyes reminded her of endless skies stretched across wide-open spaces. Tanned, chiseled features were softened by a growth of brown stubble a few shades darker than his collar-length sun-kissed hair. His gaze flickered over her body—over the sports bra and skin-tight yoga pants she wore only when she was at home by herself—before returning to her face, reflecting blatant appreciation.

"Didn't mean to startle you, miss. Your bush needs trimming." His resonant Texas drawl distracted her a second before the bizarre remark registered.

"My *what*?"

He blinked as if her question surprised him. A moment later, a dark stain flooded his face all the way to his cheekbones. She'd never seen a man blush so deeply. "The bush next to your fence," he quickly clarified. "I, uh, thought you might not have the right tool."

"The right tool?" Jen followed a line of western snap buttons down the front of his faded chambray shirt, past a Texas-sized belt buckle, and only then did she notice the gas-powered hedge trimmer clutched in his left hand.

She jerked her attention up to his face. He meant the *shears*, for God's sake. How had she missed the fire engine red *lawn tool?* And he had to have noticed where she looked to start with. Flustered, she shot back. "Do you make a habit of strolling into people's backyards looking for work, cowboy?"

His answering smile landed like a punch to her solar plexus. God help her, a dimple, visible even through the scruff. "Only if I leave my horse at home."

Jen bit her lip to keep from bursting out laughing, from nervousness as well as his awful joke, which for some reason she found hilarious.

"Sorry for bustin' in on you." He didn't look sorry. If fact, he appeared irritatingly aware that she found him attractive. "Should've introduced myself right off. Logan Hardt." He stuck his hand out and engulfed hers in a warm clasp. Rough callouses pressed against her palm, setting off a sizzling current that raced up her arm, igniting her dormant libido. Was this some latent physiological response tied to her body's ticking clock?

She jerked her hand away and self-consciously brushed at limp strands of hair around her face. With no make-up and sweaty from working out, she had to look dreadful, and couldn't be making a good first impression on the neighbor, if that's what he was. She'd never seen him before, and she would've remembered. "Do you live around here?"

"Nope. Texas." He hooked his thumb over his belt in a time-honored manly stance, still holding the hedge trimmers with the other hand. "My family owns a ranch...a little ways southwest of Fort Worth."

Could this get any weirder?

"So you came all the way from Texas to Atlanta to perform lawn services?"

The dimple reappeared, making her heart perform another flip. "To be in a friend's wedding, actually. Troy McKinney. He and his girlfriend, Celeste, live next door."

Logan indicated with his chin to the right, perhaps assuming she didn't know her neighbors.

"Yes, I've met them." Jen recalled the couple had gifted her with a plate of chocolate chip cookies while she'd been moving in. She had intended to return the favor and bake something, but got busy with work and ended up having cupcakes delivered with a thank-you note.

"They're having the wedding at their house, and they asked me to help get the back yard into shape." Logan gestured with the shears at the evergreen shrubs spilling over the fence, which the real estate agent had declared to be a privacy feature. Now the reason for his interest in her bushes became clear. She couldn't believe he'd blushed. Most men would've howled with laughter at her misunderstanding. Logan didn't act innocent, however. *Gentleman* was the word that came to mind.

Gentleman or not, he was still intimidating, and a stranger at that.

Jen scratched her head, perplexed by the instant attraction. "I suppose I could make the shrubs look a little neater. I've been meaning to find the name of a good lawn company, but I haven't had a chance yet."

"Troy said you just moved in—"

"A month ago. I didn't realize the bushes bothered them." Her neighbors must be conflict avoidant, so they'd sent an emissary. Equipping a cowboy with a hedge trimmer seemed a bit much.

Logan lifted one shoulder in a casual shrug. "Like I said, I can take care of it."

"No need to put yourself out. I'll call someone today." Afterwards, she'd get moving on finding a donor. In fact, if she could dictate a description of the perfect specimen, he would look very much like this man.

Freckles bounded up, barking. Had Logan been a squirrel, the dog would've met him at the gate. As it was, an intruder could slit her throat and empty the house of valuables before the silly mutt noticed he was leaving.

"Some watchdog you are." Jen grabbed the checkered collar when the dog rushed at Logan. "Hush, now. Sit down."

Freckles dropped her butt on the bricked patio a femtosecond before leaping up to continue her fierce barking, forcing Jen to tighten her grip on the collar.

"I'm sorry. She won't bite you."

Logan knelt and set aside the hedge trimmers, then held out his hand for Freckles to sniff, without the least bit of apprehension. "Hey there, pretty girl."

His drawled praise fluttered across Jen's heartstrings. An irrational reaction, considering he wasn't talking to *her*. The dog shied away, being her usual cautious self. Finally, she risked venturing close enough for him to stroke her head and scratch behind her silky ears.

"Soft and sweet, just what I figured."

Freckles rolled over and presented her belly.

Revealing a submissive nature to an Alpha might work for dogs—for humans, not so much. Being soft and sweet was a sure way to invite hurt, and didn't get a woman very far in the professional world either.

He left off crooning to the dog long enough to deliver another heart-stopping half smile. "Name?"

"Jen"—she took a quick breath to restart her heart—"Chandler."

"Fancy name for a dog."

She refrained from smacking her forehead, but couldn't stop the eye roll. She would've realized he meant the dog if he hadn't thrown her off balance with that dimple. "*Her* name is Freckles."

"Pleasure to meet you, Jen and Freckles." Still rubbing the dog's head, Logan sailed right past the embarrassing moment. "She's got pretty spotted markings on her face and legs. I can see why you named her Freckles."

Jen recalled her mother had scoffed at the name. *Freckles? Why would you name a dog something silly like that?* "You don't think it's silly?"

"Nah, it fits." Logan patted his knee. Freckles rested her paw where he indicated, gazing up at him adoringly. "Good girl." He ran his fingers through the dog's fur, and Jen's skin prickled at the thought of being stroked by those strong, calloused hands.

Amazing, how fast Freckles had warmed up to Logan. The rescue dog was typically reserved around men—one thing they shared in common, and for good reason. Men in their past had abused their trust. But animals had a sixth sense about people, and Logan had passed the test.

Equally surprising, Jen didn't feel uptight. Being attracted to a man would usually put her in a state of nervous anxiety. Logan exuded calmness, and it must've rubbed off on her. She'd been wondering how she would find a donor, and this handsome, chill, dog-loving cowboy had strolled into her back yard. What were the odds of that?

The breeze lifted a lighter strand of his hair and blew it across his forehead. The men she knew used special products to achieve a tousled, windblown look. Logan didn't appear the type to bother with styling his hair. He was naturally blessed with thick, wavy locks—another nice trait, along with his impressive height and rugged build.

Her watch buzzed, reminding her of what she *ought* to be doing instead of standing around daydreaming about what his progeny might look like. In her mind's eye, she saw a sandy-haired baby boy with dimples.

While Logan watched quizzically, she turned off the notification. "I'm sorry, I have to go. Conference call in fifteen minutes."

"Want me to take care of those hedges?"

If he was so insistent, who was she to argue?

"Okay, fine. But I'll pay you for your trouble."

He stood, all six feet something, and looked down at her with a half-smile. "Are you hirin' me?"

Hiring him? *Maybe.* In fact, the more she thought about it, the more appealing the idea. Logan had no ties to her. In fact, he'd soon be on his way back to Texas. Strange as it seemed, he could turn out to be the perfect donor.

Her stomach knotted at the thought of his reaction if she told him *why* she might want to hire him. After that faux pas, when she'd misunderstood his question, then looked at his crotch! *Geez!* He would think she was a kook. She couldn't discuss things like sperm count—yet. First, she had to get to know him better.

"Mr. Hardt...*Logan*." She supposed they needed to be on a first name basis. "I'd like to have your number, if you don't mind, so I can get in touch with you to arrange payment. And...I might need another favor."

Jen swiveled her office chair around to the computer. The glass-topped desk and fossilized redwood base she'd paid a fortune to move looked out of place in the paneled library. She generally preferred modern architecture, but this dear old house had called to her. Her parents had advised against investing in what they deemed a "crumbling old mansion," which had only strengthened her resolve to buy the place. They understood the value of a house, or a business, or even fine art. But the value of something you loved just because? No, and she'd never figured out how to increase her value in her parents' eyes. Success helped, but that wasn't why she worked so hard. She put in long hours to make up for what was missing in her life. So, she could accept being lonely and having no one to love, or she could do something about it.

Yesterday, she'd entered Logan's number into her phone, but still hadn't worked up the courage to call him. Outwardly, he appeared to be a perfect candidate, plus he seemed like a nice guy. Then again, she could make a list of nice guys who were anything but. Before she called him and took this any further, it wouldn't hurt to do a little research.

It was entirely possible he'd made up that story about Texas and the ranch, and was a worse liar than her last boyfriend, who'd slept around, all the while pressuring her to marry him.

"Who are you, Logan?" She typed *Hart Ranch Texas* into the Google search bar. Drilling down through the results, she discovered an article on historic Texas ranches. Near the bottom, she spotted a listing for Double H Ranch owned by Katherine Parker Hardt and her children, the descendants of Jacob Ross Hardt, who'd taken over the reins from his ailing father in 1871. The original holdings had been divided among descendants, some who still lived there.

Jen grabbed a notepad and started jotting information. *Not Hart, but Hardt, with a d.* Was Logan from this distinguished Texas bloodline? Her father would be impressed. Not that she cared, but he had ridiculed her decision, saying she would know nothing about the donor's family. Should Logan check out otherwise and be agreeable, she might bear a child whose ancestors had lived on the same land for generations. More than her father could claim.

She rocked back in her seat in amazement. No wonder Logan sounded so proud when he said he lived on a ranch. Not just any ranch—his family's ancestral homeland for more than a century. Having that kind of connection to the land and to the past had to give him a strong sense of belonging. She'd never lived in one place long enough to feel connected to it.

Additional searching didn't turn up much more information. Logan didn't even have a Facebook page, or if he did, it wasn't under his name. That didn't mean he wasn't who he said he was. Intuition told her to move ahead, as planned. She trusted her instincts when it came to business, and that's exactly what this was — purely business.

Jen picked up the phone. The best way to find out more

about him, without tipping her hand, would be to suggest a casual dinner. It wouldn't be a date, not in the traditional sense, more like doing research on a prospective employee. Her heart pounded as his phone started to ring.

He might've given her his number, but wasn't really expecting her to call. She hadn't been at her best. Then again, he'd been the one to trespass and startle her. This would've been so much easier if she'd met him at a business luncheon. Running into Logan at one of the trendy cafés she frequented? She pressed her lips tight to keep from laughing.

"Hello?" His deep drawl provoked an attack of goose bumps. At least he hadn't said *howdy.* She would've dissolved into giggles.

"Hi, Logan. It's Jen Chandler."

"Jen, I'm glad you called."

"You are?" That sounded breathless, too eager. She needed to keep this casual. "I, um, just got around to calling back. Had tons of emails to read…"

She scrolled through her unopened messages and noticed one from her father's assistant. He might want to know her plans for the upcoming holidays, so he'd asked Abby to contact her. He also had his secretary send out her birthday cards and purchase gifts, and Jen wondered if her father even remembered the day anymore.

"Too bad you have to work," Logan's remark dragged her out of her musings. "I've been goofin' off. We went for a drive around Atlanta and visited the aquarium."

"I've heard that's nice."

"You haven't been there?"

"Not yet."

"One to put on your bucket list. What about the history center and Margaret Mitchell's house?"

"Never been to either, but I love *Gone With The Wind.*"

"Then we should go. I'll see what else is on the schedule while I'm here. If you have time, you can come along."

Well, he'd made that super easy, asking her out first. She

hated being stuck with strangers, but touring Atlanta with Logan actually sounded like fun, and it would give her a chance to get to know him. On the other hand, trying to interview him with his friends around would be difficult, not to mention awkward.

She gathered her courage. "How about if we go to dinner instead?"

"Dinner? Sure, that'd be great." He sounded genuinely pleased.

Jen released a breath of relief, so far so good. "Tonight, say six? Just walk over, I'll drive." That way, if things didn't work out, she could bring him back early. "We can go somewhere simple, casual." Probably best if she kept this low-key. She wanted him to feel comfortable, and he seemed like the laid-back sort. "Whatever you're hungry for, just ask your friends to suggest a place. I'm not picky." If she didn't like the fare, she could order a salad.

"I'll ask...and I look forward to seeing you." The suggestive tone set off warning bells. He'd gotten the wrong idea and thought dinner was a prelude to dessert—in bed. She might fantasize about him, but actually have sex? Out of the question. When it came to physical intimacy, she closed up quicker than a clam.

"Wait!" She could find out what she needed to know another way, by hiring a private detective. "I just remembered something I need to do. We'll have to take a rain check on dinner."

"That's too bad."

His disappointed tone gave her pause. If she blew him off now and came back later with a request for him to be a donor, he might turn her down, and she'd lose what could be a golden opportunity. She hadn't offered anything more than a meal. They didn't have to sleep together to make a baby. At the right moment, she could explain everything. One step at a time...

"No, forget what I said. I'll just rearrange things. We can still do dinner."

His silence worried her. She propped her elbow on the desk and put her forehead in her palm. *Great. Just great.* He now thought she was a ditz and was reconsidering accepting her invitation. "Logan, are you there?"

"I'm here. What changed your mind?"

His question caught her off guard. "Changed my mind?"

"You asked for my number, asked me to dinner, but you seem…unsure."

Jen's heart tripped. He'd seen through her bluff, and on the phone no less. She could lie and say she wasn't a bit hesitant and make up some story, but she had a feeling he would know she was lying. "Oh. Well, I've never asked a stranger out. I guess I wasn't sure if you were a bona fide good guy, or dangerous."

"I could be both."

She smiled into the phone. Another thing she liked about him, his sense of humor. "Just remember, I have a permit to carry a gun." She had nothing of the sort. In fact, she didn't even own a firearm. But he didn't know that.

"What caliber?"

"Colt 45." Wasn't that a handgun? Or was it a malt liquor? Belatedly, she typed *popular handguns* in the search bar; she should've known better than to talk guns with a cowboy.

His chuckle sent off another round of shivers, not the bad kind, or maybe these shivers *were* the bad kind, the worst kind. "I'll be there at six."

Chapter Two

Logan followed Jen through a dingy restaurant only slightly larger than a tack room. Smoke and grease oozed out of every nook and cranny, mingling with the pungent smell of barbeque sauce. The best joints generally looked like a breeding ground for food poisoning, and he hoped that was true in this case. Crank-out windows on three sides of the shack were open. Still, it was hot in here compared to the mild temperatures outside.

"How about this?" He indicated the only open booth. "We'll have a window."

The clicking of her high heels stopped. "Helpful if the place catches fire."

His lips tugged at her dry retort. Jen's sharp wit was the second thing about her that attracted him. The first thing was her sweet ass. Unfortunately, when he'd strolled into her back yard and saw her bent over, his brain had shut down, and he'd blurted that stupid remark about trimming her bush. A wonder she hadn't told him to go to hell. He'd managed to redeem himself after befriending her dog.

Chowing down on barbeque seemed like a good way to relax and get acquainted, or that's what he thought when he asked Troy to suggest a good place for ribs. Jen had said she preferred something simple and casual. She looked dressed for neither, fitted black top, electric blue skirt, chase-me heels…he didn't recall telling her she'd be dancing with the stars. He wouldn't complain though, she looked as fine in that outfit as she'd looked in those stretchy pants, which had distracted the hell out of him.

She drew her skirt beneath her and scooted onto the bench, past a torn spot where the stuffing spewed out. "Do you suppose the ripped vinyl is a deliberate design feature?"

"Absolutely." He set down the tray with the food they'd collected at the counter, and slipped onto the opposite bench. Someone had halfheartedly swiped a damp rag over the faded plastic tablecloth after the last guests had vacated. "And the greasy checkered tablecloth. That's a nice touch too."

Jen angled a look at the unfinished wall. Hanging, slightly tilted, was a framed vintage print advertising repair services on Woodies. Someone had cut off the illustration of the old station wagon. She arched an eyebrow, conveying her thoughts with one small gesture. His grandmother did that. Pops had called her "saucy." The word fit Jen as well. "Let me guess. This place is on the top ten for the most charming redneck restaurants?"

"Even better…" Logan leaned on his arms, grinning. "Rated number one by Atlanta goat ropers."

Jen's dark gaze gleamed with amusement. She didn't break eye contact, not even when her watch glowed with some new notification, as it had numerous times on the way over. He hoped her rapt attention meant she was as fascinated with him as he was with her. Something about her intent study reminded him of the way his father looked at a horse he was thinking about purchasing.

Logan exhaled a dry laugh. Jen wasn't buying anything, and he wasn't selling. He might consider giving it away though, if she kept looking at him like that.

She'd shed her black all-weather coat, which had pink-lipped kisses stenciled all over it. Not many women could manage to make something ridiculous appear classy, further evidence she'd be an interesting date. "You should've warned me about the dress code. Sadly, I don't own a western shirt or Wranglers." She eyed his get-up. "I do have boots."

"Are they stenciled with pink lips?"

"Do you have something against pink lips, cowboy?" She gave him another arched look.

"I love pink lips." He stopped short of saying he'd be happy to sample hers. Later, maybe, depending on how well things went. He hadn't expected her to ask him out on a date. That had been a surprise, albeit a nice one. She had seemed a little anxious, but if she didn't ask guys out on a regular basis, she might've panicked, thinking he'd see it as an invitation to jump her bones. Honestly, the thought *had* entered his mind, more than once, but he didn't intend to start anything. He'd just have a nice dinner with a pretty woman who'd flattered him with her invitation. Beyond that...

He couldn't think *beyond that*. Too many obligations waited back home for him to get tangled up in a long-distance relationship, and he didn't do one-night stands, although he might make an exception in Jen's case.

She turned the paper boat holding her turkey sandwich. An odd choice at a rib joint, but some people didn't care for ribs. At least she wasn't vegetarian. He hadn't thought to ask before suggesting barbeque.

"Let's hit the chow." Logan rolled up his sleeves.

She stared pointedly at his forearm. "That's some tattoo, it looks like an Indian on a horse."

He couldn't tell whether she was impressed or turned off. She didn't wrinkle her nose, so he took it as a good sign. "A Comanche warrior. My mother's family can trace their roots back to Quanah Parker. You might've heard of him; he was a famous half-white chief."

Jen's eyes widened. "You're part Native American?"

"The blond hair and blue eyes give it away every time."

Logan teased, and basked in the glow of her awestruck expression. Things couldn't be going better on a first date, she was impressed with his ancestry, she appreciated his sense of humor, and she looked as if she wanted to take a bite of *him* instead of her turkey sandwich.

At this rate, they just might end up in bed, which surprised him. Usually, he was the one standing around watching, while women hit on Huston and Clay. His friends described his brothers as "chick-magnets." If they were here, Jen would've no doubt asked one of them out, an annoying thought. Clay had assured him that he could score more often if he'd half try, but he wasn't into casual sex and one-night stands. Still, he wouldn't fight too hard if Jen decided to seduce him.

Jen couldn't keep her mind on her food with Logan flashing that dimple and giving her heart palpitations. He'd been flirting nonstop, and clearly thought this was going somewhere. She hoped he wouldn't be too angry when he discovered the direction.

"You aren't eating," he pointed out. "Would you rather go somewhere else?"

She could imagine where he might suggest, and it wouldn't be a restaurant. "Oh, no. This is fine. These small, undiscovered places usually have the best food."

He glanced around. "Looks like it's been discovered."

True enough. Customers were packed into the tiny hole-in-the-wall, wearing jeans as well as business suits. Logan fit in just fine, yet even she didn't look out of place. "I've only been in Atlanta for a little over a month and haven't had time to research restaurants." *Or sperm banks, for that matter.*

She poured her lite beer into a plastic cup and took a sip. Thank God Logan couldn't read her mind. That didn't make it any less embarrassing when she considered what she was about to do—interview a potential sperm donor without him realizing her purpose. A first date offered the perfect set-up for questions, as couples were generally eager to learn more about each other. Might as well start with his eating habits.

"You like barbeque?"

"Oh yeah. I got a weakness for slow-smoked ribs." He turned his plate around, tore off a rib, and bit into it.

She couldn't stop staring at the colorful tattoo along the side of his muscular forearm. The exotic design intrigued her, even though she didn't care for tattoos, and she had the oddest urge to trace the image with her fingertips.

A scar that snaked the length of Logan's thumb looked like an old injury. From barbed wire? Oh, for God's sake. No one used barbed wire anymore. There were more humane ways to keep cattle in a pasture. Weren't there? She didn't know squat about cows *or* cowboys.

Jen sneaked a peek at her smart watch. She'd need to learn all she could about this cowboy, and fast. Based on her ovulation-tracking app, she'd reach her peak fertility late next week, and he'd be gone shortly thereafter.

After wiping his hands on a paper towel, he selected a spicy sauce and squirted it over the remaining ribs. "How about you? What kind of barbeque do you like?"

"Oh, just about anything. Turkey, chicken…" She didn't want to appear picky after telling him she didn't care, then ridiculing his choice in eating establishments. Not everyone appreciated sarcasm, but he'd exhibited a well-developed sense of humor, so he knew she was teasing, and she found his rapid-fire banter refreshing.

"You want to taste one?" He held out a meaty rib. "They're great."

She smiled, shaking her head. "Thanks, but no. I don't eat smoked ribs. Not because I don't like them — they taste wonderful — but they're loaded with fat. Plus, charred meat isn't good for you. It contains carcinogens."

Undaunted, he cleaned the rib of meat before responding, "How can something that tastes so good be bad?"

"Lots of things we like aren't good for us."

"So you avoid them?"

"For the most part."

He unrolled another paper towel. "My grandpa had a saying: *Everything in moderation.* It's a good philosophy. One I try to live by."

Clearly, Logan didn't overindulge in rich food and drink, or he wouldn't look like a cover model for *Cowboys & Indians*.

Jen picked up her dry turkey sandwich. "If you can practice moderation, it's a good philosophy with regard to eating."

"Pops wasn't just talking about food."

Logan had a point. She might be missing out on some of life's pleasures because she didn't think she could manage them. For her, it was all or nothing. Strict adherence to self-made rules kept her urges in check. She clung to comfortable routines. One might call her slavish in her devotion to her schedule. Logan's laid-back personality would be a nice counterbalance to her obsessive tendencies.

"Tell me more about your family." She left the door open, purposely. Whatever he chose to share would be revealing.

"That could take all night." His slow smile made her lips tingle. All night didn't sound half bad. "I'll give you the condensed version so you don't get bored. I have four brothers: Jake is the oldest, he's a sheriff's deputy; Clay helps out with the horses in between rodeos; Huston just got discharged from the Army; then there's me; and my younger brother, Austin…"

Jen filled in the blank with a guess. "Rides broncos?"

"No. He works at a fancy restaurant in Fort Worth."

"As a waiter?"

"Sous chef."

"That's impressive."

"Glad you think so. Austin gets a load of crap from my brothers about wearing apron strings."

Macho guys could be jerks. "What do *you* think about it?"

"I think he's a damn good cook. Wish we could afford him on the ranch."

Jen smiled, pleased by the response. "You love your little brother."

"I love all my brothers. We give each other a hard time, but in spite of the bullshit we dish out, we know we can count on each other." Logan's matter-of-fact proclamation set off a twinge in Jen's chest. She'd never experienced anything approaching what he took for granted. How different would her life have been if she'd had that kind of familial devotion?

She brushed aside the pensive thoughts and went back to her script. "What about the ranch where you live? Does it have a name?" She wondered if it was the same one she'd read about.

"The Double H."

Bingo.

"Based on your family name, I presume?"

"Actually, Double H stands for Double Hearts. As I understand, it's a play on the name. My great-great-grandfather created a brand that resembles interlocking hearts. As the story goes, he was madly in love with his wife. So much so, he made her legal co-owner of the ranch."

The romantic tidbit had little to do with what Jen needed to find out, but was fascinating nonetheless. "He doesn't sound like your typical, nineteenth century chauvinist."

Logan took a swig of beer from the can. "Mm, based on what I've heard, he was quite a character. He started crossbreeding wild horses with racing horses, and our quarter horses are descended from the ones he bred. He also imported eastern cattle to breed with the Longhorns for tastier beef."

This had to be a first, her date discussing cattle breeding. She wasn't bored though; she found everything about Logan interesting. "You really are a cowboy then."

"My father prefers the term 'rancher.' "

"What do you prefer?"

Logan's sly smile implied he found something amusing. "Most folks don't know the difference. They call any man who wears boots a cowboy, and every handgun a Colt 45."

The stinker! He was poking fun at her ignorance of both. Unable to come up with a good response, she simply ate her sandwich.

Logan finished demolishing a side of ribs. Thankfully, he refrained from talking while chewing. He pushed aside the bones and carefully wiped his mouth and fingers.

She couldn't resist. "You have good manners—for a *cowboy*."

"My mama taught me right."

"And passable grammar."

"Hey, now. I'll have you know I got A's in English."

Jen congratulated herself for not being obvious. Smart as he was, he hadn't figured out she was following a list of questions. "Did you go to college?"

"Yes, ma'am. Earned a degree from Texas A&M." Logan regarded her with a pleased expression, as if he found her interest flattering. Hopefully, he'd be just as flattered when he found out *why* she was so interested. "And got accepted into the veterinary program."

Not a dummy then.

"You're a veterinarian?"

"No. I didn't finish." Growing somber, he reached for his beer. After draining the can, he crunched it in his fist, which told her something had prevented him from completing his education, and he was frustrated by it.

"Why not?"

"Vet school is expensive." He set the crushed can aside and rested his arms on the table. Along with the scar on his thumb, he had other marks on the backs of his hands.

Perhaps he was careless, or maybe he just worked hard at tough physical labor and didn't have the benefit of a cushy job, or a trust to fund his schooling.

Jen started to reach out, but caught herself in time and curled her fingers into a fist, pretending she hadn't been about to touch him. She wasn't here to hold his hand, even if only for the purpose of offering comfort. She could give Logan something better. He needed money to finish school, which would be good motivation for accepting an offer, should she choose to extend one.

She mentally reviewed her list and checked off *Intelligence*.

"Was it something I said?"

"What?"

His blue eyes twinkled with amusement. The gene for brown eyes was dominant, but if she got lucky…"Am I boring you? Your mind wandered off."

"A woman's mind never wanders off, it just gets busy with multiple things."

"Men don't do that. We stay focused."

"You *can't* do that. There's a difference."

"Who says we can't juggle?" He picked up the plastic fork, spoon, and knife. "Want a demonstration?"

"Maybe some other time." Her mind multitasked just fine, but the interview had wandered off-topic. Despite enjoying their lighthearted banter, she wasn't on a date, and it was time to stop acting like she was smitten. Before asking him to submit to a blood test, she wanted to know more about his family. "You mentioned your grandmother, how old is she?"

"Eighty-two this month."

"Is she in good health?"

He released a dry laugh. "Miss Kate can run circles around the rest of us. If something needs to be done, she does it. She's four foot eleven and a hundred pounds dripping wet, tougher than a Texas Longhorn and just as mean when she's riled."

"She sounds ferocious."

Logan grinned. "You remind me of her."

"Is that supposed to be a compliment?"

" 'Course it is. She's great. You'd like her."

Jen responded with a wry smile. Had any other man compared her to his grandmother, she would've been ready to leave, but hearing the remark from Logan, who obviously adored his family, it didn't come across as insulting. "I'm sure I would like her. What about your father? Is he just as tough?"

"Tougher."

"And your mother?"

Logan's amused smile faded. "She died three years ago...after fighting cancer for over a year."

All it took was one look at his face to know he still grieved deeply. Jen ached for his loss. Her problems with her parents seemed, in contrast, insignificant. At least she had both parents. "I'm sorry. It must've been hard losing your mother like that."

"It was…still is."

"Has anyone else in your immediate family had cancer?" Genetics often played a role.

He shook his head with a perplexed frown. "No other women in her family died from breast cancer, as far are we know. Her folks are pushing ninety and still going strong. Her grandparents lived a long time too. Dad said he couldn't remember Mom being sick before the cancer got her."

Jen recalled he'd talked only about his paternal grandmother. "What happened to your dad's father?'"

Logan rubbed the back of his neck and frowned. "We lost him ten years ago."

"Heart attack?" That would be her guess.

"No, Pops was healthy as a horse. A drunk ran into his pickup head-on."

Jen covered her mouth, stifling a gasp. "Oh no! How awful!" What a senseless tragedy, both losses, senseless and inexplicable. Two of the people he loved most in the world, gone... She couldn't find words. Sympathy was too mild term, and she wasn't good at expressing emotions.

Logan peered out the window into the darkness. Possibly he was also uncomfortable with articulating deep emotions, and it was fine if he didn't want to go there. After a moment of silence, he brought his attention back to her. "Tell me about your family."

Her family? That topic wasn't going to make the conversation lighter. Nevertheless, he had the right to ask questions, considering the grilling she'd been giving *him*.

"I didn't know my grandparents well. My dad's parents were gone before I was born. My maternal grandmother lived the longest. She was eighty-nine when she died, but she lived in a retirement home in Florida so I didn't see her often."

Logan leaned forward, bracing his arms on the table, his attention fully on her, which was uncomfortable, yet immensely flattering. "What about your parents?"

"Mom's retired and living in Hawaii. Dad stays as far away from her as possible; he has a place in New York." Jen couldn't see a reason for going into any more detail than that. She wasn't here to talk about her relationship with her parents, a topic generally off-limits with friends, much less someone who was still pretty much a stranger.

"Any brothers or sisters?"

Jen squirmed in the spotlight, though she couldn't fault him for showing an interest in her. Her last date had talked about himself endlessly, without prompting. "I'm an only child."

Logan regarded her sympathetically. Clearly, he projected his perspective onto her life, assuming she'd missed out on what he valued—a big, close family. She could hardly miss something she'd never had. She *was* a little jealous though.

Uncomfortable with the direction of the conversation, Jen flipped it back on him. "I've lived a boring life. I'm sure you have fascinating stories."

He gave a laugh. "Fascinating? That's assuming a lot."

She didn't think so, not with his good looks and that country-boy charm. He could have any woman he wanted. Taking another sip of beer, she pondered over how to discover another important fact. Was he sexually active? If he slept around, he was more likely to carry venereal disease. "What about your, um, relationships? Have you had many?"

Surprise flashed across his face, followed by momentary confusion, then a pleased smile played around his mouth. "Why do you want to know?"

Jen was glad she'd shed her coat, as hot as it was in here, and getting even hotter by the minute. She'd never chased a guy, much less probed into his sex life, but she couldn't explain her interest without spilling the beans, which she wasn't ready to do. "Just curious," she muttered.

His smile turned wry. "You want names and dates?"

She choked on her beer, and burst out coughing.

Logan handed her a paper towel, then he got up and went to the counter to ask for a glass of water.

He'd list his conquests? He had to be joking. Even if he wasn't, she had no desire to know *all* the details.

He stood beside her until she was able to catch her breath. Maybe he thought she'd need CPR. Attentive *and* considerate, whether simply a reflection of good manners or true compassion, both were appreciated. What a pity those traits weren't inherited.

When she'd first met him, she had been tempted to write him off as nothing more than a good-looking cowboy. But Logan was more than that. Far more. She knew many men with more impressive resumes, but liked none of them half as much as she liked Logan. She decided then and there that *liking* the donor would be added to her list of requirements.

She waved him back to his seat. "I'm fine. Just a tickle," she rasped.

Her watch vibrated. She checked the read-out before turning off the notification. *Darn.* She'd forgotten to chart her basal body temperature this morning.

"Something important you need to do?" he inquired, looking curious.

Not choke to death? Still struggling to stop coughing, she shook her head and said without thinking, "It's my…ovulation tracking… notification."

Glancing up and seeing his perplexed frown, she realized her blunder and formulated a quick explanation. "This new smart watch is designed especially for women, with lots of useful apps." She blathered on, hoping to distract him with talk about her job. "I'm testing the beta model. The company is one of our agency accounts."

"That's impressive. What else does it do? Notify you when you ought to have sex?"

His quick mind had latched onto the implications, which meant he could easily figure out why she might be tracking ovulation.

Shaken, but not about to show it, she kept her tone businesslike. "Actually, yes. It involves a number of factors that are recorded, and taken into account in the calculations. The app issues a notification when there's a window of opportunity for conceiving."

"Is the window open?"

Oh, but she'd stepped in it this time!

Bits and pieces of other conversations drifted over— sports talk, fishing, Little League, a favorite movie—

nothing as interesting as what they were discussing. She prayed the people around them weren't eavesdropping.

Logan's skeptical look told her he either didn't believe her, or thought she was wacky. But everything she'd told him was the gospel truth; she'd just left out the part about her own personal interest, as it seemed a little early to be approaching him about being a donor. On the other hand, with a donor chosen, she could be pregnant by the time the new app hit the market.

She still needed more facts about Logan's background and his physical condition, but she couldn't get that information without asking, and what was the point in pursuing it if he wasn't interested? "I offered to test the app because I'm planning to have a baby through artificial insemination."

No laugh. No wry smile. No look of disbelief. Before, he'd been pretty easy to read, but now, when it mattered most, he gave her no reaction, or he was darn good at hiding his thoughts when he wanted to. His gaze dropped to her half-finished sandwich. "You'll need to eat more."

Of all the things she expected him to say, a remark about her eating habits wasn't one of them. "Of course. I know that. I'm just not very hungry at the moment."

Her secret was out, so she might as well get around to what she'd brought him here to discuss and hope for the best. Leaning over, she pitched her voice low enough not to be overheard by the people around them. "There's only one problem...I need a donor."

Chapter Three

"She wants me to donate my sperm!" Logan whisper-shouted into the cell phone. He didn't want to wake Troy and Celeste, who were in the bedroom next door, and the walls weren't thick like that stone fortress where Jen lived.

His brother Huston howled with laughter in his ear.

"It's not funny." Logan started across the guest room, which was twice the size of his bedroom at home, with twice the furniture. He caught his shin on the corner of the bed frame, swore at the sharp pain, and hopped around the bench pushed up to the end of the bed. He dodged an armchair and limped to the paned window.

He could see over the bushes he'd trimmed to the house next door, Jen's ivy-covered castle. Did she plan on filling it with children? She didn't seem the Mother Hubbard-type. In some ways, she fit the image Troy had painted of her — cool, poised, and aloof. She worked hard at hiding her vulnerability, but it was there, lurking behind those big brown eyes. Although he never would've guessed in a million years why she'd asked him out.

"Tell me about the date," Huston urged.

"Not much to tell. We went to a barbeque joint, ate, and

talked." Logan scratched his head. He couldn't figure her out. The way she'd looked at him, like she was hungry for something. Not sex, exactly. He'd seen that look before and could recognize lust. No. Jen's need went deeper.

"How did she lead up to the big question?"

"She told me about her ovulation app."

"Her *what?*"

"She tracks her ovulation on a smart watch."

Static noise came from the other end of the line— Or was Huston snickering?

"Sounds like an interesting conversation."

"It was." With a sigh, Logan leaned his arm on the window frame while he studied the neighboring house. He could explain the physical attraction, but he couldn't explain why he felt drawn to Jen on a deeper level. Maybe it was the rebound effect after being dumped, and then having a pretty woman hit on him.

Light spilled from the back of her house onto the brick patio, and he watched as Jen's dog darted outside. Not long afterwards, Jen herself came into view. She crossed the patio and ran into the yard wearing what looked like a baggy sweatshirt and sweatpants, with her hair pulled back into a ponytail — still looking as cute as a doodlebug.

Freckles jumped as she lifted something into the air. They played tug-of-war with what looked like a carcass, but was probably a stuffed toy. Jen's carefree laughter drifted upward, triggering every male impulse inside him, including the one that made men act like idiots.

Logan turned away from the window. Jen wouldn't appreciate him butting in on her private time, and she'd think he was a weirdo if she caught him spying on her. "She asked a bunch of questions," he said to Huston. "I'd thought she was interested."

"She *is* interested — in your sperm!" His brother snort-laughed.

"Honest to God, I'm hangin' up if you don't stop."

Logan fisted his hand against the wall. He ought to know better than to call Huston to talk about this. His brother couldn't have a serious conversation with an undertaker.

Who else would he call though? Huston was his closest sibling, but more than that, he was his best friend. Only thirteen months apart, they'd been inseparable growing up. The two of them, together, had taken all the shit their older brothers could dish out, and everyone else for that matter. Usually though, he was the one listening to Huston brag about his latest conquest, or moan about getting rejected by a girl he had his eye on. Not that Logan was bragging, because Jen's request defied categorization.

Women had chased him.

Women had used him.

Women had sworn to love him forever—then cheated on him.

But until now, no woman had asked him to give her the means to make a baby without any involvement beyond jerking off. Jen hadn't offered a different option. The way she'd phrased it, made it sound like she expected him to deliver his contribution in a mason jar, like a rancher might do with bull semen.

"What's the big deal, Logan? Guys donate to sperm banks all the time."

"She's not a bank."

"Didn't you say she offered you twenty grand? Sounds like a bank to me, and she's giving you a better rate."

"How would you know? Have you donated?"

"No, but a friend of mine did. He only made fifty bucks. She must think you've got prize-winning semen."

"I'm seriously going to kill you when you get here," Logan muttered, sinking down onto the side of the bed. He braced his elbow on one knee, bracketing his forehead with his hand. His stomach had been tied in knots ever since Jen had dropped that bomb on him after dinner. At least she'd waited until he'd finished his ribs. "She wants me to get a blood test first; says she can pull strings with some lab downtown…and she asked for a medical history on our family."

"Did you tell her about crazy Aunt Minnie?"

"Get off it, man. I'm not in the mood."

His brother went silent. Finally. This wasn't a joking matter.

"You like this woman…Jen? Is that her name?"

"Yeah."

"But you just met her."

"Listen to you, the guy who falls in love when a woman buys him a drink."

"Who said anything about love?"

Logan straightened. Love sure as hell wasn't on *his* mind. Getting laid? Maybe. He'd congratulated himself on snagging the interest of a smart, beautiful woman clearly out of his league. But it wasn't *him* she was interested in; it was only what he could offer as a reproduction source. If some lawn guy with the right physique had shown up instead, she would've offered to buy *his* sperm.

"*My point* was how fast you decide you're interested in a woman," Logan explained. "I met Jen. I liked her. We went to dinner. That's all there is to it. Except for the…you know."

"Okay, so things didn't work out the way you expected. You're leaving next week anyway. Why does it matter?"

"It matters because it's worth twenty grand. That'll get me through a year of vet school." He hated that Jen's offer tempted him. They would be turning something mysterious and sacred—making a child—into nothing more than a business transaction. Not to mention his intense discomfort with the idea of fathering a baby he'd never get to see. If he accepted the deal, he had to sign a contract waiving his parental rights and agree not to contact Jen or the child.

"Why not ask for fifty grand? That'll get you through two years."

"Seems mercenary to haggle over the price."

"She's the one who wants to cut a deal."

Logan scrubbed his fingers through his hair. At last, he'd met a woman who sparked his interest *and*, he'd thought, seemed interested in him. As it turned out, Jen only cared about his physical characteristics and genetic makeup, like that was all he had to offer. But Huston had a point. Rather than letting her offer bother him, he should consider it, and weigh the advantages against the disadvantages.

"Yeah, maybe you're right."

"I'm always right."

"Even if I do agree, it's selfish to keep the money. Dad needs it for a new barn. Besides, I can't leave and go back to school, he needs my help."

"He won't take your money, and you're not that important."

Logan smiled at his brother's quick comeback. Huston was right about their father; he wouldn't take charity, even if Jesus wrote him a check. "You're just saying that to make me feel less guilty about going back to school."

"Somebody has to shrink that big head of yours. We can manage without you."

"You can't get rid of me that easily. I'll set up my practice in your front yard."

"Deal."

Drawn back to the window, Logan looked out again, but found Jen had gone back inside and turned the lights out. Troy and Celeste had gone to bed too. In fact, they'd seemed as if they couldn't wait to bid him goodnight. He envied them; they made love look easy. Everyone assumed he hadn't married yet because he wasn't ready. At twenty-seven, that wasn't the case. He just hadn't found the right woman.

"She might not think I'm worth fifty grand."

"Sleep with her, then ask."

Logan smiled, his sense of humor returning. "Great idea. I'm sure afterwards she'll double her offer, and then some."

"That's the spirit. When I get there next week, you can tell me what she decided you were worth."

"Like hell. We won't be discussing this again…and don't tell Dad." Logan could imagine his father's explosive reaction. "How's he doing?"

"Not so good this week. Yesterday was their anniversary."

"Ah shit." Logan rested his forehead on his arm. "I forgot. Should've called him."

"You can talk to him tomorrow. I told him you remembered, but that you were out and couldn't call until late."

Logan closed his eyes. He could count on Huston to cover his ass. "Thanks."

"No problem. Now get some sleep." His brother's voice held a ragged edge.

Logan didn't doubt their father had been a bear, and he was usually the one who dealt with his dad's low moods and rampages, acting as a buffer between his father and his brothers. He couldn't recall exactly when he'd become the appointed peacemaker, but he was more than ready to turn that role over to someone else…if he could be sure blood wouldn't be spilled.

"Yeah, you get some sleep too." Logan disconnected and dropped his phone on the bed. He undressed down to his briefs, all the while mulling over Huston's suggestion that he sleep with Jen…his brother's idea of a joke, or partly a joke. Even so, the thought held more appeal than it should. Sleeping with her wouldn't be wise.

Then again, getting her into bed *would* be a nice side benefit to go along with the money, and he had to admit it would also go a long way in soothing his smarting pride. He could make it a condition for his agreement. Why not? She'd probably turn him down. Then he wouldn't have to wrestle with the moral dilemma.

Chapter Four

The watch on Jen's wrist vibrated. She rolled over, groping on the bedside table for the digital thermometer. According to the midwife, she had to take her temperature before getting out of bed, sitting up, or even talking.

The mattress bounced as Freckles leapt down, ran to the bedroom door and whined. Jen raised one finger up in the air to indicate she knew the poor thing had to go out, but she needed a moment. Not that Freckles cared, or even knew what she meant.

Still bleary-eyed, it took her longer than usual to enter her temperature. "All right," she said, getting up to go to the kitchen. She let the dog out and then went straight to the coffee machine. She couldn't think without coffee.

Setting her laptop on the counter, she pulled up the ovulation tracker. The app on her watch synced with her phone and her computer — beautiful thing, technology. Inconsistent menstruation made establishing a pattern for her difficult, but by tracking her temperature and other bodily functions over a six-month period, the app had enough data to predict when ovulation would occur, right down to the precise moment she should introduce sperm to egg. If everything worked out with Logan as she hoped it would, she could try to get pregnant as early as next week.

She let Freckles in through the sliding door and put the dog's bowl on the floor—a cup of high-protein dog food recommended by the vet—before going to the refrigerator to get an organic yogurt for herself. She grabbed a bottle of spring water and washed down a prenatal vitamin, along with Chasteberry, an herb that helped normalize the functioning of the ovaries. By staying fit and eating the right things, she was doing everything she could to prepare her body for carrying a healthy fetus to term.

Her smartphone buzzed and she grabbed it, hoping it was Logan, but her assistant's name appeared instead.

Darn.

"Morning, Angela," she said cheerfully.

"Hey, Jen, I thought you were coming in early so we can prepare for that pitch?"

Double darn. She'd totally forgotten, and she didn't want to leave for work in case Logan showed up.

"I'm sorry, I have to work from home this morning. I'll send you a list of what we need, and if you could gather it..."

"No problem. Oh, almost forgot. You got another invite to a baby shower. What's that, the fourth this year? They're putting something in the water, I swear."

Jen dropped the empty plastic bottle into the recycle container. "Maybe I should try drinking from the fountain instead of bringing in bottled spring water." Making a joke about the office fecundity was better than letting the news get her down.

Angela laughed. "Do you want me to pick up something for Carrie? I think she's having twins. Girls."

"No, I'll get the gifts." Jen didn't add that buying presents for pregnant co-workers helped her combat the tendency to be jealous. "Just send me an email with where she's registered."

"Will do."

"Thanks a million." Jen pulled up her reminders and entered a note to buy baby gifts, and purchase her assistant a gift card to her favorite restaurant, a well-deserved thank-you, even if it wasn't nearly enough.

Her watch lit up, letting her know it was time for a workout. Once she downed a cup of coffee, she'd change out of the over-sized sweatshirt, her favorite pajamas, into her exercise clothes, and afterwards, get a hot shower. Going through her routine would calm her nerves. She wouldn't be as worried if Logan hadn't gone quiet on the way back from the restaurant. After they'd pulled into her driveway, he'd agreed to consider her request and said an awkward goodnight.

He might still turn her down in spite of all the money she'd offered him. Maybe she should've offered more. Fertility treatments averaged five grand a pop, and *in vitro fertilization* was a whopping twenty grand. There were organizations where men donated free sperm. *Ugh!* She wasn't gambling on her baby's future. Why take a chance, when she could secure a donor to her liking? After researching the process, and watching close to a hundred videos on DIY insemination, she'd found a midwife who'd agreed to come over and help. Doing this at home would be far less stressful than going to a cold medical facility.

Her phone trilled with a special ring, indicating it was her mother. *Gosh, it must five in the morning in Hawaii.* Jen debated responding with a message that she couldn't talk, but then her mother would call back anyway and berate her for not calling more often…

"Hi, Mom. You're up early."

"You know I can never sleep past four. I'm surprised I caught you. I usually get your voicemail."

Jen refused to accept the guilt. She already carried too much around to take on more. "You almost missed me today. I'll be on my way to work in a minute." Not a lie, exactly. She *would* be working on something in a minute. "What's up?"

35

"Did your father happen to mention that he went in for a stress test?"

Stress test? Didn't doctors order those when they suspected heart problems? Jen swallowed the lump that rose in her throat. "No, he didn't say anything."

"I wouldn't know about it, except his secretary called to get your new address, and she 'accidentally' happened to mention he was at the doctor, so of course, I had to ask."

"What were the results?"

"He was still at the doctor when I talked to her, and you know he won't tell me, even if I ask."

Her mother was right, her father wouldn't tell anyone, and he would be appalled to find out either of them knew anything about it at all. She wanted to kiss Abby for letting the news *accidentally* slip. Otherwise, they wouldn't hear a thing...until after her father dropped dead. "I've been after Dad for years to start exercising and stop eating red meat."

"He won't listen to you. He doesn't listen to anyone."

Jen closed her eyes and sighed. The same old complaints about how cold and distant her father was, and how he'd never learned to show affection. Her mother hadn't been much better, but now that she was in therapy, she seemed to think she could psychoanalyze the rest of them. "Thanks for letting me know about Dad. I'll give him a call."

She spoke with her father on the phone less often than they exchanged emails, which was maybe once a month. But if she waited for him to make the first move, it might be too late. After her conversation with Logan, her parents' health had been on her mind. Seeing the grief on Logan's face when he'd talked about his mother and grandfather had, quite frankly, shaken her. "How are *you* feeling?"

"I'm healthier than ever. I've taken up hula, which relieves stress. You should try it. I'm sure there must be places there that teach it."

Hula? Seriously? Jen rolled her eyes. She liked yoga just fine, and it didn't require a grass skirt. "I'll look it up, Mom."

"You should take better care of yourself and not work so hard."

That was rich, coming from one of her Type A parents. "Need I remind you, Dad's picture is next to the definition of workaholic in the dictionary? And you were at clients' beck and call when you had your interior decorating business."

"What are you saying? That I wasn't there for you?"

Jen frowned. What in her voice implied rebuke? As much as she'd longed for her parents' attention growing up, as an adult, she'd moved past being wounded. "No, I'm saying I learned my work ethic from you and Dad."

"I hope we taught you more than that."

Her ultra-confident mother sounded uncertain, as if she wanted reassurance. This conversation had taken a strange turn. Possibly, her mother felt a twinge of guilt about being distracted while her daughter was growing up, or maybe she had woken with an indefinable sense of loss. Time was something neither of them could get back.

Jen had no idea what to say. Replaying *if only* wouldn't change the past. She'd withdrawn emotionally years ago, when her parents hadn't been there for her at a time she most needed their love and support. Intense psychotherapy had helped her work through her anger and resentment, but she hadn't been able to overcome all the issues she'd spent a lifetime developing.

For the sake of her yet-to-be-conceived baby, she had to *try*. Her mother and father would be her child's only grandparents, and they wouldn't be around forever. "Mom, what are you doing for Christmas?"

"Aren't you coming out here?"

"I've just started a new job, so I don't have much vacation time, definitely not enough to fly to Hawaii. Why don't you come here and spend Christmas with me? I've got lots of room, and I'd love to show you the new house."

"Oh..." Her mother's disappointed sigh came through loud and clear. "I was counting on you flying out here. I'm in charge of the bridge club party the week before Christmas, and I'm hosting a big New Year's bash for my book club."

"Then fly out Christmas Eve, and just stay a few days."

"What about your father? He might decide to come down to see you Christmas Eve."

"I doubt it." Her father hadn't mentioned his plans, but he'd worked too many Christmas Eves to count. Even though he'd supposedly retired, he still kept busy with his investments.

"Let me think about it," her mother replied. Which meant, no, she wanted it her way.

Jen wasn't up to arguing.

Freckles suddenly went wild, barking and running around like mad. As the dog raced toward the sliding glass doors leading out to the patio, Jen turned to look.

Logan waved from the other side of the glass.

Elation surged through her. She hadn't scared him off.

He grinned and gave her a thumbs-up, and her heart leapt into her throat. *Oh my God! Did that mean yes? Yes, he'd do it?* She caught herself throwing a fist punch into the air, and fumbled with the phone.

"Jen? Jen, are you there?" Her mother's voice sounded faint.

She put the phone back to her ear. "Sorry, I can't talk now. Somebody's at the back door."

"Who is it?"

How could she answer, yet avoid getting into another pointless argument? Her mother had already made it clear she didn't approve of the method Jen chose to conceive, and instead had advised her to find a husband first. Her ovaries would wither while she waited for the right man to show up, and she wasn't sure she had the temperament to put up with him if he did.

The thought occurred to her that before this week she'd never considered a man like Logan.

This morning, he'd shed his western button-down for a

gray Dallas Cowboys t-shirt, which revealed more of his impressive physique. She bet he honed those lean muscles working at his family's ranch, rather than on equipment in a gym.

"Looks like a cowboy," she answered, finally.

Freckles darted back and forth, baying, and at the same time, wagging her tail. She knew her new boyfriend was at the door and was eager to greet him.

"Did you say *cowboy?*"

"Gotta go, Mom. Love you." There, she said it first. Jen ended the call before her mother could feel awkward about responding in kind.

As she reached for the lock, she issued a command to the dog. "Sit!"

Freckles tried. Her backside touched the marble floor for about a second before she jumped up again. She panted, her tongue hung out, and her sleek body trembled with excitement. Jen knew exactly how the dog felt.

She pulled open the door. "Come in but watch out, you might get attacked."

Logan flashed another grin. "Best offer I've had all year."

His arm brushed hers as he stepped inside. Her body hummed with energy, the way she usually felt after a workout, not before, and the current was different, like DC instead of AC. Even the air shimmered with sexual awareness.

While Freckles jumped on her new best friend, Jen shut the door, using both hands, because they were shaking. She needed coffee...food...sex— Oh, *hell* no! Crawling into bed with Logan Hardt would screw up what had to be a business arrangement, *strictly* business.

She ventured meeting his impossibly blue eyes, which delivered another shock to her system and set off a rapid fluttering in her chest. He held her gaze long enough to confirm the intense attraction wasn't one-sided.

Switching to defense mode, she turned her attention to

the dog, pulling Freckles away from clawing at Logan's jeans. *Trying to tear them off?* She and the dog were on the same wavelength. "Get down."

"Sit." Logan's request, delivered in a low, but firm, voice, had a miraculous effect.

Freckles dropped to her haunches...and remained seated.

"Why, you! You're making me look like a bad mommy." Jen bit her lip. Wrong thing to say, as it implied she lacked parenting skills. If she didn't pull herself together, she would mess this up long before she got Logan's signature on a contract.

She made her way to the counter and pulled open a drawer with individual coffee pods arranged by strength and flavor. "You drink coffee?"

"Does a duck swim?"

Jen threw an amused glance over her shoulder. "Depends on the duck's mood, I suppose."

"This duck is in the mood." The teasing glint in Logan's gaze sent a shiver through her. "For coffee," he added with a straight face. "Strong as you got."

She took down two mugs from the cabinet above the coffeemaker. "French roast all right?"

"Fine with me." Logan squatted down to pet the dog. Freckles trembled at his touch. She had never behaved this love struck with anyone else, although it shouldn't be surprising Logan had that effect on females. The combination of rugged handsomeness and gentle strength acted as a powerful aphrodisiac. He'd offered to make a list of his previous relationships. Joking, of course...or maybe not. He hadn't followed through, probably because the list would be a mile long.

"Do you take anything in your coffee?"

"Milk."

"That's the way I like it too."

"Is that so? That makes three things we have in common, we're both up early, we like our girls sweet, and our coffee strong." His voice came from behind her. He was so close, if she turned, she could put her arms around him.

Bad idea. This had to be a business arrangement or it wouldn't work. Actually, they had little in common.

"I think girls should be strong and coffee sweet." She added a spoonful of sugar to her mug. "So... Have you given some thought to my offer?"

The coffeemaker hissed, releasing the last of the steam, while Jen held her breath.

"Thought about it all night."

She poured a dollop of milk into both cups, trying to keep her hands from trembling. "And?"

"I'll do it."

The vise squeezing her heart released and she exhaled. She hadn't realized — or maybe she had — how much she wanted him to say *yes*. Normally, she relied on facts, not emotions, which were notoriously misleading. For some reason, she trusted her gut instincts about Logan.

Calm down. Additional facts were needed before she could be certain. "Can you go to the lab for the blood test today?"

"Yes, ma'am. I'll get whatever doctors' records you want. Transcripts. Resume. We've got a family history online, if you'd like to read it."

Was he mocking her?

No, he appeared serious. She responded with equal seriousness. "Yes, I'd be interested. I think it's a good idea to know as much as possible about the donor." She chose the word *donor* rather than *father*. Thinking of Logan as her baby's father made it too personal. She offered him the coffee mug.

He cupped her hands, trapping them against the warm ceramic, then gazed into her eyes, too deeply for her comfort. "I agree. We ought to get to know each other. I'm curious too."

His touch warmed more than her hands, so she couldn't blame the hot coffee. Her lungs constricted, making it hard to breathe. No, she couldn't let this attraction fool her into thinking of him as anything other than a donor, or this wouldn't work. There could be no loose ends and no regrets when he left.

She pushed the mug into his hands and pulled out of his grasp. "What are you curious about?"

"You."

Whether he was genuinely interested or just trying to get into her pants, she wouldn't let him close enough to find out. "What do you want to know?"

"Everything you're willing to tell me."

"I'm financially stable, have a Master's degree, and if you'd like, I can provide character references."

"Why are you being so touchy? It's not an unreasonable request," he said, his voice remaining calm and friendly, which put more knots in her insides.

"I'm not being touchy. I just don't understand why you feel the need to know *everything*."

He seemed sincerely astonished. "Because you'll be the mother of our child."

Jen's knees gave way, and she had to grab the counter for support. He made it sound like they would be raising a baby together. He couldn't be serious, or if he was, he hadn't thought through the complications, which were terrifying to imagine: the turmoil, the uncertainty, the inevitable rejection her child would experience when Logan got around to marrying some other woman and starting his own family. He had to let go of the idea that he could insinuate himself into her life and play daddy whenever it was convenient. She'd grown up in a dysfunctional home and wouldn't let anyone put her child through that kind of heartache.

"*My* child, you mean. You agree to waive your rights, all your rights, or this deal is off."

Some raw emotion flashed in his eyes, only for an instant. Hurt? He didn't know her well enough to be emotionally invested. He was probably just pissed off because she wouldn't go along with whatever game he was playing, which she could figure out if he wouldn't stand so close. At least he was frowning now, instead of giving her those puppy dog eyes.

"I didn't mislead you about this arrangement," she reminded him.

The muscles in his face tightened. "Waiving my rights doesn't mean walking away without a thought. I won't sleep well at night if I don't feel comfortable with whoever's raising a child I helped make."

"This isn't a child you're giving up for adoption. It's spermatozoa—" Jen sealed her lips. Too late, the crude remark had escaped. She knew she was being unfair. Blame it on fear.

Still planted directly in front of her, Logan took a leisurely sip of his coffee. "You've got your conditions. I've got mine."

Conditions? What more did he want from her? She'd offered him a big check. Based on the hard set of his jaw, if she didn't give a little, she would lose him...as a donor...and that was all she needed from him, nothing more. He was making this more difficult than it needed to be.

She practiced deep breathing. Anxiety would spiral into panic if she didn't get it under control.

Logan took a step back, as if sensing her need for more space. He couldn't know why, but he'd already demonstrated that he was surprisingly perceptive, and was more thoughtful than most men she'd known. Maybe that's why she hadn't expected him to make demands. Then again, what did she really know about him? Not enough to have too many expectations.

Jen circled behind the breakfast bar. Putting a slab of granite between them should help her think more clearly. "How long is this list of conditions?"

"It's a short one. First, go out on a date with me this coming weekend. Second...we make a baby the old-fashioned way."

Chapter Five

*L*ogan hummed the song *Country Girl, Shake it For Me* while he waited for Jen to buckle her seat belt. Even the rain couldn't dampen his good mood. Damn, she looked good in that dress. The soft material hugged her curves from the waist up, and fell loosely around her hips to mid-thigh. Nothing covered her tanned legs except a pair of strappy sandals.

After his blood tests had come back normal — in a blazing two days, thanks to Jen's lab contacts — she'd agreed to go out with him and also to give some thought to his second request. Which meant he had a chance to convince her to sleep with him. He tried not to think too much about being paid afterwards and leaving. Those were bridges better crossed once he came to them.

She frowned at the steady rain pounding against the windshield he'd cleaned that morning. The wipers thwacked as they moved back and forth, flinging water. Pulling down the visor, she grimaced at the mirror.

"Just look at my hair."

He did as she asked. Her shiny brown hair hung past her shoulders in a simple, but elegant, style, which suited her. "Looks fine to me."

She tucked some of her hair behind one ear, revealing a gleaming silver disc in a small lobe he had a burning desire to nibble. "It would have to rain."

"Pretty much guaranteed. I washed the truck." He pulled the F150 to the end of her driveway. Not sure where to go, he shifted into park. The truck's engine dropped to a low grumble.

Four years ago, he'd bought the broken-down vehicle for next to nothing, and his brothers had helped him get it running again. On his first date with Jen, he'd ridden in her shiny Mercedes Benz. The turquoise pendant hanging from a silver chain around her neck looked like it was worth more than his truck. The differences between them couldn't be more glaring. That might be why she was pouting. She didn't want to be seen riding around ritzy Druid Hills in a run-down pickup truck.

"Where to?"

"Wherever you'd like."

Definitely pouting. She didn't push out her lower lip and cross her arms over her chest like his five-year-old niece did, but her chilly politeness lowered the temperature in the cab.

Logan refused to be discouraged. He wasn't sure what had spurred him to ask for more time with her. Getting her into bed had been his only goal when he'd headed over to her house. He came up with the additional prerequisite after she'd greeted him at the back door, looking adorable in an over-sized sweatshirt and with bedhead.

Maybe the smell of coffee, which he associated with homey images, had triggered the crazy daydream. Waking up next to her, the dog curled up at end of the bed. Sharing coffee on a cool morning. Bantering with someone who got his sarcastic sense of humor, and even better, dished out her own brand.

The physical part was easy to understand. Attraction pulled at both of them. He'd seen it in her eyes when he'd brushed up against her, and again when he'd cupped her hands with his. As for domestic thoughts, she hadn't given him a sign she entertained any, just the opposite, in fact. She kept referring to him as "the donor."

He knew why she did it, to keep him at arm's length, but he didn't like the distance. In fact, he disliked her insistence on making this exchange impersonal. Something in him—a bone-deep, stubborn streak that infected the men in his family—had reared up. He would drag Jen out of her comfort zone and force her to acknowledge him as a man, not just a reproduction tool. By the time he got her into bed, she'd want to be there as much as he did.

"Let's go dancing."

"Dancing?" She reacted like he'd suggested they deliver a calf in the fields.

"It's moving your feet to music."

She gave a fluttering eye-roll he found charming. "I know what dancing is."

"Good. Do you know how to line dance?"

"You're kidding, right?"

"I'll take that as a no. I could teach you. It's easy."

Her expression turned incredulous. "You want to go to a country and western bar?"

"Sure. You know of one?"

When she didn't answer right off, he wondered if he ought to suggest drinks and dinner and be done with it.

No. He wasn't giving up. He wanted her to learn how to have fun, because she'd obviously missed out on that particular lesson.

"Oh for goodness sake, if you insist..." She put a perfectly shaped fingernail between her teeth, and sighed. "I've heard of a place downtown...I don't know much about it, but it's supposed to be the popular spot for wanna-be cowboys."

"Alrighty then, we'll go there."

She eyed his dashboard. "I assume you don't have GPS on this truck?"

He snapped his fingers. "Dang. Forgot to tie the homing pigeon to the roof before I left Texas."

"Sounds messy..." Jen tapped something on the screen of her phone. After a moment, a male voice with an Australian accent told him to turn right.

Logan left the driveway and followed the instructions, although he didn't trust the Aussie tour guide any more than he did the female version. They'd as likely guide him to the middle of a cornfield and tell him he'd reached his destination.

Jen set her phone on the seat, and then swiped the screen on her wristwatch. She'd been wearing the watch every time he saw her, and he wondered if she even wore it to bed. Worse, would she be checking her notifications over his shoulder while he tried to get her pregnant?

He was pretty sure he'd lost his mind to agree to this.

Once more, he tried to get her attention. "What do you usually do when you go out?"

She looked up immediately. Ah, not as distracted as she wanted him to think. Maybe she used that watch to avoid talking to him. "I don't go out that often. When I do, it's usually for cocktails or dinner, maybe a movie or a play, sometimes a concert. Mostly client entertainment."

"How about when you're on a date?"

"I don't go on many dates."

He found that hard to believe, with her pretty face and a body that could put him into cardiac arrest. "Just business? No fun?"

"No time to goof around."

And there she went, looking at that glowing watch again.

"You too busy checking your ovulation to goof around?"

She gave him an arched look, which told him she didn't appreciate his humor. He knew she did, though maybe just not *that* particular zinger. "We have a big pitch coming up. I thought my assistant might be sending me a message."

At least he'd gotten her talking.

"Troy said you were a vice president or something?"

"Senior partner. They call it vice president to impress the clients."

A high-powered job…maybe she really did work all the time. Had she given much thought as to how a child would change her life? "When you have a kid, you'll need to goof around more."

That remark earned him another raised eyebrow. "I'll make time. I'll set up play dates."

He didn't laugh, because she didn't appear to be making a joke. She couldn't be serious though, that wasn't spending time with her kid, a play date was arranging for *someone else* to spend time with her kid. "My dad took me fishing and taught me how to ride a horse. My grandpa showed me how to shoot, and took me hunting. Our family went on float trips and camping trips, and my mom hosted scouts and helped with the 4-H Club. What did your parents do with you?"

The way she stared at him made him wonder if he had hair growing out of his nose.

"*Do* with me? They sent me to private academies and I spent summers at camp." She delivered the comment without a trace of emotion.

Logan's chest began to ache. In other words, her parents couldn't be bothered. No wonder all she could come up with was *play dates*. "You deserved better than that."

She turned her head to look out the side window. "What are you talking about? My parents gave me everything I ever asked for."

Yeah, everything except what she needed. The tug in his chest got stronger, and he considered beating his forehead against the steering wheel to distract his heart and keep it from wandering off and settling in Jen's lap. He was a damn fool if he let himself care for this woman. His heart wasn't what she wanted.

"*Turn right and continue right…*"

He didn't need the reminder. He'd determined, at a relatively young age, to stay on the right path after his three older brothers raised enough hell for all of them combined. He disliked being forced into a mold as much as they did, but seeing his mother cry over their antics had shaken him to the core. He had vowed she would never cry over him. He sure hoped his mom was keeping busy in heaven and not paying attention right now, because he knew without asking what she would think of this deal he'd struck with Jen. He still wasn't sure why he'd agreed, but he didn't want to think about it too deeply. Not tonight, anyway.

The bright Atlanta skyline shone above the trees, which he'd been surprised to see in a big city. Even so, this wasn't the country. He couldn't see the stars, and the air smelled like exhaust fumes. Visiting cities was fun, but he didn't want to live in one. Jen, on the other hand, looked like a city girl from the tips of her manicured fingers, to the ends of her pedicured toes. They couldn't have much in common, which was another reason to avoid letting this attraction drag him into a relationship that wouldn't last, even if she allowed herself to consider the possibility. That didn't stop him from being curious about her. "You mentioned your dad lives in New York City. Did you grow up there?"

She glanced down to where she'd put her hands in her lap. At least she didn't raise her arm to look at her watch, a minor improvement. "No, we moved around a lot, until my parents split up when I was in high school. When I was younger, we lived all over the United States. I've worked in London, Paris and Tokyo."

Jen had been all over the world, which made him feel like a hayseed.

"Our family took vacations in the western U.S., mostly Colorado. I've been to maybe ten of the fifty states. Never been out of the country, except for Mexico. Have you lived in big cities mostly?"

"And in the suburbs. We lived in Druid Hills when I was ten. I loved all the trees and the old houses. It's a nice place to raise a family, which is why I moved back." Leaning against the seat, she stretched out her legs and seemed to grow more comfortable.

He imagined running his hand up one long, slender calf, and had trouble keeping his eyes on the highway.

"What about you?" she asked. "Have you lived in the same place all your life?"

"Other than going off to college, I've stayed on the ranch. I imagine that sounds pretty boring to someone who's been all over the world."

"Actually, it sounds wonderful. Living in a place that was home to generations of your family must give you a strong sense of belonging."

Was that why she looked so wistful, she didn't feel like she'd found home? Logan tried to put himself in her place, and couldn't. As much as he envied her experiences, he wouldn't trade his life for anyone else's. "Yeah, I guess you could say that. I grew up with lots of family around, and always felt like I was a part of something. Something bigger than me."

"That sounds nice. I wouldn't have a clue about living on a ranch." She sighed, and it seemed a yearning sound. It could mean nothing, but then again, she'd brought up the possibility of living on a ranch, not him. The thought of taking her back to Texas made him way happier than good sense should allow.

"If you could adjust to moving every couple years, you could adjust to living on a ranch."

"Are you kidding? I don't know one end of a cow from the other."

"Trust me, you'd figure that out real quick."

Her smile took his breath away. She was even prettier when she let down her guard and enjoyed herself. That's what she needed, someone to help her find her way to having fun and loving life. He pictured a scene of them together, in the future, with their kids running around th—

"You have arrived at your destination."

"Shit!" Logan jerked the wheel, the tires squealing as the truck bounced into a parking lot. Jen's phone, which was lying on the seat next to her, went airborne and she grabbed for it. Rather than dodge pedestrians, and a long line of cars and trucks, he swerved to the left and found an empty space at the far end.

That was a close one. He'd allowed his mind to wander, and not to a safe place, when he should have been paying attention to his whereabouts. He had no business dwelling on an unlikely future with someone like Jen, or even considering shouldering more responsibility than he already had, considering he was in no position to settle down. Not until he'd finished his education and gotten his life back on track.

He opened her door to help her out of the truck, and caught her surprised expression.

"That's sweet. Old-fashioned, but sweet."

"Haven't other men opened doors for you, or offered you their arm?"

"Let's see…" She pursed her lips as if in thought. "Mm, no."

"What kind of men have you been hanging out with?"

"Men from this century," she said, and slipped her arm through his.

They started across the parking lot toward a brick building with a set of doors painted black, and above the entrance hung a pair of metal longhorns, nothing else about the place suggested *honky-tonk*.

The two men standing in line in front of them were dressed like cowboys, the kind that didn't do real cowboy work. One of them threw a curious glance over his shoulder, and then turned all the way around. "Well, *hello…*"

The fake cowboy gave Jen no more than a passing glance, and it hit Logan, the man was eyeing *him* with interest. He didn't react, but he sure as hell began paying attention to his surroundings. Being so focused on Jen, he hadn't really noticed the people around them, mostly men, there as couples or in groups, and some were embracing.

When the ogler turned back around, Logan shot a quick glance in Jen's direction to see if the obvious had registered with her yet. Based on what she'd said earlier, she hadn't been here before, so maybe she didn't know she'd brought him to a gay nightclub.

She lifted up on her toes and craned her neck to peer over the heads of the men lined up in front of her. "Looks like a long line."

Her remark offered him a convenient excuse for leaving without offending or embarrassing her. "We can try somewhere else?"

"I suppose, but if we drive around aimlessly, we might end up somewhere we'll get mugged. If this doesn't appeal to you, we can just grab a quick bite and get back early."

Her sweet-as-sugar smile set off his bullshit alarm. Jen knew exactly where she'd brought him, and had done it hoping to cut their date short. Maybe she wanted him to think she was a lesbian so he wouldn't hold her to her agreement to sleep with him. He had nothing against gay men, or women, but he'd bet his right nut Jen was as straight as a fence post.

If he took her home, she'd brush him off, saying she needed to get work done, then come up with some equally annoying excuse for not sleeping with him. He could try to find another place…or he could call her bluff.

"We're here, might as well see what it's like inside. I'm in the mood to dance." He grabbed her hand and dragged her inside behind the crowd.

The strobe lights and loud throbbing music would've been enough to send Jen running, but being pressed on all sides by hot, sweaty bodies put her into a full-blown state of panic. Her hands got clammy, her heart raced and her mouth turned dry, next would come the lightheadedness. If she didn't get out of here, she'd faint. Crowds were the worst. *Damn*. She should've guided him to a teahouse.

Logan slipped his arm around her waist and drew her against his side. Odd, his touch didn't trigger the urge to recoil, even though being touched usually made her anxiety worse. His embrace seemed more protective than possessive, which might explain why it didn't bother her. Whatever the reason, having his arm around her helped, and the suffocating pressure on her lungs eased. She huddled closer and tried not to look around.

Why had he brought her inside? He couldn't *want* to be here. He wasn't gay — no way — but he hadn't balked, as she'd predicted he would, being a macho cowboy. Why, he hadn't even blinked when the hunk in front of them had turned all the way around and batted his eyelashes.

Logan put his lips to her ear. "You picked a popular place."

"And hot…"

The looks the male patrons were sending Logan's way heated up the already steamy room. Overpowering odors—smoke, booze, and men's cologne—made her stomach churn. If she could hold her breath without losing consciousness, she would.

"How about a drink?"

"No, thank you." She longed to break away and run, right out the door. That was still an option.

"Let's dance."

"No—" She didn't even get the chance to get out *thank you* before he hauled her onto the packed dance floor where the patrons were forming lines, like clones, in their skin-tight jeans and cowboy hats. No manure on *their* boots. Most of the men had removed their shirts and were bare-chested. Why, she didn't know, and didn't care, she just wanted out. Logan didn't seem to notice her discomfort, and he positioned them in front of a black giant and his small-boned, pale-skinned partner, whose eye makeup looked better than hers.

"Time to get down and get Footloose!" The jarring shout came from the loudspeakers, and the music swelled.

Jen's lungs withered like deflated balloons, forcing her to suck for air. She drew in another breath, and yelled to be heard above the music. "I don't know this dance."

"Watch. Do what I do." Logan began to bob and clap, and in front of them, another line formed. Surrounded on all sides, she could either go along, or push her way out. Which would be more humiliating?

"I been workin' so hard. I'm punchin' my card..." As the words to the song started, everyone around her, still clapping, began to move, and few were looking her way. She would fake it until she saw a chance to slip through the crowd and find a restroom where she could hide out, and stay holed up long enough for Logan to get tired of being hit on, and then he'd surely take her home.

Gritting her teeth to keep them from chattering, she clapped along. The only way she'd make it through this would be to focus on something other than her spiraling anxiety. She honed in on Logan's steps: *sideways, one foot behind the other, then front to back...heel, toe...* His movements were sure and fluid, like he'd been born knowing how to dance, and he was graceful for such a tall man, and had the fancy footwork down pat. She hadn't danced in years, prayed she wouldn't fall on her face.

Her attention remained riveted on Logan, and imitating his steps, which took her mind off the crowd. As long as people didn't push or press against her, she'd be okay. She imagined being surrounded by a force field that kept everyone else away, everyone that is, except Logan. He'd slipped into her inner circle without even trying.

On the way over, she'd revealed things she hadn't intended to reveal. She couldn't afford to allow him any closer, even if she couldn't resist being drawn to him, in ways she hadn't been drawn to any other man. It had to be because she'd chosen him to father her baby. Rather, to *donate* what she needed to have a baby. He'd been the one to start in with this father stuff, but she refused to buy into it. Couldn't. Logan Hardt would leave just like every other man she'd counted on. The best thing for both of them would be a clean break. No ties, no regrets.

He threw her a grin, kicking his leg up and hitting the side of his heel with his hand. She mimicked the move and returned the infectious smile. The steps repeated. Once she had the moves down, she relaxed and started to enjoy herself.

As a child, she'd loved to dance, although her lessons had been in jazz and ballet, not country dancing, but learning the basic steps wasn't all that different. Her training came back, along with her natural ability to pick up on complicated patterns, and this wasn't all that complicated. One dance merged into another, this one to *Boot Scootin' Boogie*, which proved to be easier to follow. She didn't miss a beat when the music shifted again, and the deejay announced the next song, *Watermelon Crawl*.

As the swinging rhythm began, Logan launched into a seductive strut. At one point, he reached out and drew her back a few steps. "Like this," he said, swiveling his hips in a blatant imitation of the sexual act. A burst of sparks raced across her skin. *Hot damn*, he was a good dancer...and good dancers were also good in bed, or so she'd heard.

She hadn't given him a firm answer about whether she would, as he'd put it, "make a baby the old-fashioned way." Her plan called for keeping things above-board and as impersonal as possible, and she couldn't get much more personal than taking him to bed. Still, just thinking about being in bed with Logan sent excitement coursing through her, and it wasn't the nervous kind. Sexual excitement wasn't something she experienced very often, which she blamed on her inability to get past the kissing phase without freezing up.

What would it be like to kiss Logan? She studied his mouth. If he pressed his lips against hers, would they feel soft or firm? Did he favor lip-sampling kisses, or swirling tongues?

As if he could read her mind, he moved closer, leaned in,

and brushed a quick kiss on her mouth, which was partway open because he'd surprised her. The shock took her breath away. She stumbled, but caught herself, and flushed with an equal mixture of longing and embarrassment. He should've warned her that his lips carried a high-voltage charge.

His eyes never left hers as he performed another suggestive gyration.

An ache started low in her groin, throbbing in time to the music. With a knowing smile, he stepped back, clapping, then dropped to his knees and thrust his hips. Her pulse accelerated and her breasts swelled, the push-up bra felt much too tight and rubbed agonizingly against her stiff and aching nipples.

The devil was seducing her on the dance floor!

He came to his feet with effortless grace, and the man who'd eyed him outside moved behind him, mimicking the erotic motion. Logan didn't act as if he noticed, but she sure as hell did. *Okay, it was just a dance, but still!*

Jen executed a half-turn and backed up, almost touching Logan's crotch when she rotated her hips in time with the music. A glance over her shoulder revealed the surprise on his face, a split-second before his eyes blazed. The heat in his gaze fueled the fire racing through her veins.

He wanted her, she wanted him, and for the first time in years—no, for the first time in her life—she wasn't afraid. At least, not at the moment, she wasn't. She was sure she'd feel differently once they were alone and he started removing her clothes. His request might not seem like a big deal to *him*, but *she* had a problem with intimacy, especially with a man she intended to send away.

The fake cowboy behind Logan didn't get the message, or simply didn't care. He moved closer, rather than backing off. At the same time, other dancers began to crowd around. No one noticed she happened to be in the way.

The crowd pressed against her—hot and sweaty, and reeking of beer and cigarettes. Hemmed in on all sides, she couldn't escape. Overpowering odors clogged her nostrils, and she struggled to breathe. Her heart lurched into a wild, erratic rhythm, and she feared she was having a heart attack, or that's what it felt like.

A cry for help stuck in her throat.

Logan grabbed her hand. She clung to him with the desperation of a drowning person grasping a rope, and he slipped an arm around her waist and hauled her off the dance floor. "I've had enough. Let's go."

Thank God!

He pulled her through the crowd and didn't stop until they'd burst through the door and were in the parking lot. Outside, the air smelled like car exhaust, which was an improvement, in her opinion. At least she could breathe again.

The aftermath was almost as bad as the panic attack, with bouts of uncontrollable shivers, interspersed with hot flushes. Embarrassed, she tried to pull away, but Logan didn't let go. Gently, he drew her closer. "You all right?"

"Yes. Yes, I'm fine."

"You look pale. I was worried you might faint."

He'd noticed? For a time, she had lost sight of him in the crowd; or maybe she'd lost sight of everything but her own fear. She should've taken him somewhere else, but that wouldn't have been any better. Agreeing to go dancing had been a mistake.

She fanned her face with her hand. "My God, it was hot in there."

"Yeah. *Hot* is one word for it." Logan secured his arm around her waist and escorted her to the truck.

She didn't have the strength, or the desire, to push him away, being too wrung out and exhausted. "Do you mind taking me home?"

He opened the passenger door, his expression turning thoughtful. "Does that happen often, or only in crowds?"

Jen tugged her skirt down as she slid onto the seat and grabbed the seat belt. Her anxiety disorder was the last thing she wished to discuss with Logan. He'd already gotten too close. He made her want things she shouldn't, and confiding in him would only make their inevitable parting more painful. "Nothing happened. I just started feeling a little sick with all that smoke."

Excessive smoke *did* bother her, not as much as all the people that went with it, but she hadn't lied. With years of therapy, and practice, she'd learned to manage her anxiety, mostly by avoiding the triggers—like the one she'd just experienced. On the drive home, she managed to relax a little, and, to her relief, he didn't question her or try to chat. Maybe he'd decided to drop this absurd effort to get to know her.

He pulled into her driveway, put the truck in park, and turned off the engine. Time to go, and she would try to forget the humiliating scene.

She grabbed the door handle. "Thank you—"

"Hold on a sec."

Her tension notched up. Logan might expect her to invite him inside to finish what they'd started on the dance floor. She wasn't up to that, not tonight, not even knowing he had the only cure for the insistent ache between her legs.

"Jen...I'm sorry."

"Sorry?" She gaped at him. An apology was the very last thing she expected, or deserved. "For what? I was the one who directed you to a gay bar." She might as well admit it, because they both knew the truth.

"Yeah, I know. But I should've brought you home instead of dragging you inside."

She searched his expression for a hint of sarcasm. No, he looked serious. Her heart constricted. He *was* serious, seriously apologizing for something that wasn't his fault. Her nervousness melted under shame's heat. "You have no reason to apologize. That whole scene could've been avoided if I'd just told you I didn't want to go out with you."

The moment the lie left her lips, she longed to call it back.

Logan's jaw hardened as if he'd clenched his teeth. He could be angry or in pain, either one would make sense, considering she'd just stabbed him with her words. Before she could find some excuse for being cruel—and there really wasn't one—he'd gotten out of the truck and started around to let her out.

She could open her own door. *Calm down, he's not a chauvinist,* her conscience chided. *He's being polite. Sit here and let him.*

The door creaked open, and she slid off the seat. He took her arm as she stepped onto the running board, then the ground. She could try to convince herself that it was nervousness and not desire that made her heart race, but another lie wouldn't make her hunger for him go away.

Her face remained warm as he escorted her to the door. She'd dealt in tricks and lies, and he repaid her with courtesy. He had every right to be frustrated, even angry. All he'd asked for was a little time to get to know her, and she couldn't dredge up the courage to give it to him.

Instead of going for her keys, she faced him. "*Please* don't pull out."

He wiped his hand over his mouth, smiling. What was so funny about...?

She caught a sharp breath when it hit her. "Oh God. I didn't mean—"

"I know."

"And you restrained yourself from remarking?"

"My restraint might surprise you."

"Everything about you surprises me."

He braced his hands on his hips. "What did you expect?"

"I don't know...a redneck. I didn't think you'd go into a gay bar, and I'm surprised you didn't kill that man for coming on to you like that. Didn't you notice?"

"I noticed. I chose to ignore it."

Jen shook her head, bemused, as her gaze traveled over his button-up shirt, nice jeans and polished boots. All dressed up, but still a cowboy. In spite of his outward appearance, Logan didn't fit into a familiar mold. He was one of a kind—insightful, thoughtful, unflappable, and entirely comfortable in his skin. Which was more than she could say for herself, being a bundle of anxiety, doubt and contradictions.

She wanted to push him away and run, at the same time, she longed to throw her arms around his neck and never let go. She feared sleeping with him, yet she ached to feel him inside her. She needed for him to leave, but she wanted to beg him to stay. If he hadn't already guessed at how messed up she was, it wouldn't take him very long to figure it out.

"Is this where we say goodbye?" He propped his hand against the doorframe, effectively penning her in. Oddly enough, she didn't feel trapped. *Sheltered* was the word that came to mind. He had protected her tonight, and she couldn't recall the last time a man had done that, if ever.

"Thank you for the evening. I did have fun." She didn't want him to think otherwise, or that her discomfort was his fault. "At least until I got hot and anxious, I had fun."

"I had fun too. You picked up country western dancing fast."

Boy, had she ever, she'd wiggled her butt like she knew what she was doing. His gaze didn't wavered, and the heat from it crept over her skin. That crazy move might've bought her a second chance. If—and it was a big *if*—she could find the nerve to meet his second condition.

She chewed her lip. One romp in bed wouldn't necessarily spell disaster, unless getting pregnant took longer than she thought. It shouldn't, if they mated at the right time, when her body was at its ripest. She could work up the nerve to have sex with Logan once and not become too attached, and that's all he'd suggested, really. He hadn't asked for more, so she couldn't be hurt because she didn't expect more.

When she put her hand on his chest, the answering flare in his eyes told her what she needed to know before she even asked. "Are you still interested in my offer?"

Chapter Six

The next day, Jen arrived at the office early. She'd closeted herself behind a closed door to get some work done. If she and Logan were going to spend time attempting to make a baby, she had to get a few things out of the way so she could relax and stay focused. Then again, when she was around Logan, she had a hard time focusing on anything else. Just thinking about going to bed with him sent a shiver of excitement through her, and if she dwelled on it for very long, she'd have the urge to touch herself...or call Logan and ask him to do the honors.

Oh, hell no. Not until she was ovulating. She wasn't doing this for the enjoyment. If she focused too much on the act, she'd freak out when they actually did it.

She hit send to answer the current email, then swiveled her chair to face the window. A good distraction was what she needed. The agency had rented space on the twenty-first floor and the skyscraper's walls were glass. When she'd first set foot into her new office, she'd nearly lost her lunch. Not only was she anxious around crowds, she was also afraid of heights. Over the past month, she'd been determined to build immunity to this particular fear, and made a habit of looking out the windows often. She'd come to enjoy the impressive view over Atlanta's downtown. However, she hadn't worked up the nerve to go over to the window and look down.

Last night, she'd managed to hold off her fear of crowds long enough to dance with Logan through three songs. Maybe it was time to try to overcome her issue with heights, at least in her own office. Steeling her nerve, she got out of her seat. She could do this.

A foot from the wall of windows, she halted, her stomach churning. If Logan's arms were around her, she might find the courage to look down. But he wasn't here, and she was about to throw up the yogurt she'd eaten earlier. She whirled around, holding her middle, sick from fear, and sickened by knowing she couldn't face it alone. Maybe one day, some researcher would invent a vaccine for acrophobia. She'd wait for the shot.

A knock sounded at the door just before it swung open. Her assistant, Angela, sallied inside with a to-go tray nestling two coffee cups and something in a small paper bag. She set it on the desk, tossing back shoulder-length springy black curls, one of the lovely physical traits she'd inherited from her Jamaican parents. "Never fear, an extra-shot almond milk latte is here, and I picked up a gluten-free egg white sandwich with goat cheese. *And* it doesn't taste like cardboard. I already ate mine."

Jen reached for the tray. "Bless you, you're a lifesaver! I appreciate it."

"Are you kidding? You called in the order and paid for mine." Angela detached her cup. "And I pass right by there on my way to work."

Jen worked her coffee cup out of the holder. She'd switch to decaf when she was pregnant. In the meantime, she'd succumb to her caffeine addiction. "I just heard from Carlos. He wants you to audition for that lingerie ad we're shooting."

"Seriously?" Angela grinned. She had a brilliant beautiful smile, another mark in her favor. The creative director hadn't hesitated when Jen had suggested her assistant for the ad. *Star quality,* he'd declared. Next stop, Hollywood.

The thought of losing Angela, who also happened to be the closest friend Jen had in Atlanta, put a twinge in her chest. "They'll hire you the instant you walk in the door."

Angela hiked the side of her fitted skirt to reveal a sleek dark thigh and a glimpse of black panties. "I've been wearing their brand for good luck."

Jen laughed. "You don't need luck. You're gorgeous, outgoing, and you're not afraid to be yourself." Which was more than she could claim. "They'd be idiots *not* to hire you."

"They wouldn't even know about me if you hadn't written that recommendation. Thank you!" Angela set down her cup and came around the desk to hug Jen's neck. She and her boisterous family had no reservations about showing affection, but Jen always felt awkward. Her uptight family wasn't the hugging type. Determined to change, she put her arms around her friend and gave her a pat. Hopefully, she could do more than pat Logan's back when the time came to put up or shut up.

"All I did was write an email."

"I know you did more than that." Angela rested her hip on the edge of the desk. "Hey, when I called last night you seemed...distracted. Anything going on?"

Jen sank back in her seat, sipping at her coffee. She'd confided in Angela about wanting to have a baby, and her plan to find a sperm donor. Her assistant had honored her confidences, and was always there to offer encouragement, which was a hell of a lot more than she'd received from her parents. She wasn't sure she was making the right decision, accepting Logan's condition. Angela would be a good sounding board. "You remember me telling you that I'm looking for a donor?"

"Oh yeah, I remember. I sent you some pictures."

Jen smiled at the reminder. "Those were movie stars. They aren't offering their sperm."

"Too bad," Angela murmured innocently, then brought her coffee cup to her lips.

"I did meet someone who might work."

Her assistant's caramel-colored eyes widened with curiosity and she lowered her cup. "Tell me more."

"His name is Logan Hardt. He's visiting Atlanta to attend my neighbor's wedding. I met him the other day. He's got excellent physical characteristics: he's tall, blonde, muscular, with a nice smile...very handsome."

"You just described Chris Hemsworth as Thor."

Jen chuckled. "He does sort of resemble Chris, but he's not Australian. He's a Texan...a cowboy."

"A *cowboy?* Jeezam!" Angela slapped her thigh. "Girl, you got it goin' on. What's he like?"

"He's"—Jen didn't know where to start—"a gentleman."

"Gentleman? You mean he's got manners?"

"I think he time-warped out of the eighteen hundreds he's so old-fashioned. He opened doors and took my arm to escort me when we went out the other night."

Angela propped on her hand on the desk and leaned in. "You want my advice? Snatch him up before somebody else does."

Jen's heart did an odd flip-flop. She couldn't— wouldn't—go there. No point in risking her heart over a Texas rancher who'd leave in a week. "I'm not looking for a man to date *or* marry. I need a sperm donor. Logan has the right genetic make-up, his blood test checked out, and I've been researching his background. It's a good fit."

Angela looked disappointed. "You asked him to donate in a Dixie cup?"

The coffee went straight up Jen's nose. She grabbed for a Kleenex, somehow managing not to spew latte. "Oh, God, stop!"

"I'm just sayin'..."

"That's not how it works."

"Yeah, well," Angela gave a dismissive wave. "I don't really want to know *how* it works. Sounds like you found what you wanted."

"I think so. There's only one problem."

"What's that?"

"He wants me to sleep with him...to make the baby."

Angela put her hand to her heart, looking horrified. "No! That's awful!" She then dissolved into laughter.

Jen couldn't share her amusement. She found nothing funny about her dilemma, which she'd admittedly created by asking Logan to be the donor. "I don't want to sleep with him."

That dried up Angela's glee. "You aren't attracted to him?"

Jen flushed. *Attracted* was such a mild term for what she felt. "No, well...yes...but that's not the point. He's very attractive, and nice, but I don't want to get involved."

"Does *he?*"

The question stumped Jen. What *did* Logan want? "I don't know. I explained that I needed a sperm donor, and I thought I was very clear about how the exchange would take place. Then he asked me out and said he wanted to get to know me better."

Angela rubbed her chin, adopting her wise-woman expression. "Yeah, he wants to get in your pants, and he knows if he plays nice, you might let him."

That explained his motive better than assuming he was actually interested in her on a deeper level. Jen ignored the tug of disappointment. "He's going back to Texas next week. I don't plan on seeing him again."

"Well if you're bound and determined to get a baby, I say enjoy him while you can."

Jen leaned back in her chair, surprised. "That's odd advice from someone who's declared she'll only sleep with the man who marries her."

Angela slipped off the desk and raised her hands. "Hey, *I'm* not the one looking to hire a sperm donor. If this Logan

Hardt is a hot as you say he is, why not sleep with him? Enjoy what you paid for."

Jen grimaced. That made it sound awful, like hiring a male prostitute. But maybe it really wasn't all that different, hiring a man for sex, or for his sperm, both were business transactions. If she thought about it that way, the interaction would remain impersonal and her heart wouldn't become involved. "Thanks for listening."

"Anytime. Good luck with the cowboy." Angela headed for the door, but once there, she paused, looked back, and delivered a saucy wink. "Look at it this way, like that country song says, you'll be saving a horse."

Holding a wedding in a back yard sounded easy enough, but Logan found out pretty quick that wasn't the case. He'd helped Troy install an arbor, because Celeste wanted to be married beneath a "leafy bower." The florist had better bring extra vines. They'd dug a pond when Troy's fiancée mentioned she wanted a water feature with live fish. After accompanying Troy to a local nursery to pick up flagstone, Logan had helped his friend install a walkway from the back patio, to the arbor and fishpond. When it came to Jen's wedding, would she have so many requests?

She would have more. He was certain. The woman had drawn up a ten-page contract that essentially said they agreed to procreate and then part ways. Something he could've stated in one sentence. He preferred not to get caught up in details, although, that tendency had gotten him into trouble in the past, so maybe Jen was smart to be specific and make her expectations clear.

Their disastrous date three nights ago had ended with an intriguing question: Was he still interested in her offer? He should've said no. For the life of him, he couldn't figure out why he'd said yes. Granted, he was hot for her, and there was the windfall he would get afterwards. But there was more to it than that, and the *more* was what scared him. If he had half a brain, he'd mute his cell phone.

Logan pulled off his t-shirt. Despite the mild temperatures, he was sweating. He wondered if it was possible to sweat out this obsession he had with a woman he barely knew.

Jen confused the hell out of him, like taking him to that crowded bar when she obviously fought agoraphobia. One of his cousins had the same problem and he'd recognized the signs. He wouldn't have taken her inside if she'd just told him about her fear of crowds. Even after she nearly passed out on the dance floor, she wouldn't admit what caused it. She swung from chilly to warm, from affectionate to distant, then reeled him in again by agreeing to have sex with him. Those were her words. Have. Sex.

Then, she hadn't invited him inside. Instead, she told him she would call. When he tried to kiss her, she turned her head, and his lips landed on her cheek. A granny kiss, that was all she'd allowed, even though she'd committed to sleeping with him at some point. Awkward didn't begin to describe how he'd felt when he'd walked away and left her at the front door.

He'd be driving home bright and early Sunday. Today was Thursday, and the wedding would take place Saturday. That didn't leave much time.

Troy filled in the spaces around the last flagstones with mulch, then straightened and stretched. He tanned rather than burned in the sun, but his shirt was just as wet. "Man, I'm done for the day. Let's grab a beer and sit down."

"Sounds good." Logan trailed after his longtime friend, traipsing over the path they'd just created and up the steps leading to the patio. He actually welcomed the physical labor, which kept him from fretting about when Jen would call. He reached into a cooler and snagged a cold bottle.

"What's this?" he asked as he examined the unfamiliar label.

"Local microbrew. Celeste loves their amber ale."

"As long as it's beer, I don't care."

"Yeah, I'm not picky either. But it is good." Troy used an opener to pop off the metal top then did the honors for Logan. "She's a real connoisseur when it comes to beer and wine…and other things I'd better not talk about."

Those *other things* had been good enough to convince Troy to leave Texas and move to Georgia.

Logan chuckled as he pulled his phone out of his back pocket. "You got it bad, Tex."

"Look who's talking? That's the fourth time you've checked your phone in the past two hours."

Logan set the phone on the table next to an Adirondack chair. "Don't want to sit on it," he muttered. He wasn't admitting he'd been about to check to see if he'd somehow missed Jen's call. *Four times? Really?* Something was seriously wrong. He hadn't been this distracted by a woman since… Wait, Jen wasn't like Kelsey, other than wanting something from him, and at least Jen was more honest about her motives. She hadn't led him to believe what they shared was anything more than a business arrangement. He'd been the one pushing for more.

He vowed to stop pushing. If she wanted to seal their bargain, she'd call. If not, it might turn out to be a blessing. He'd be out the money, but he wouldn't have to live his life wondering about a child he helped make, yet could never see.

Troy flopped into a nearby chair and took a swig. "Mm, addictive."

"That good?" Logan took a drink. The ale did go down smooth. "Tasty, but I wouldn't call it addictive."

"Not the beer. Women."

"Ah…" Logan settled against the seat back. "Yep, you're a hopeless case."

His friend nodded as if it didn't bother him to admit his dependency. He seemed proud of it even. Logan didn't intend to be so besotted, not even with his future wife—whoever that might be. Look at what happened to his father after his mother died. He'd turned hard, cold, bitter. Too much dependence on a woman could ruin a man.

"You need to bring Jen over. We'd like to get to know her better."

"So would I," Logan muttered under his breath. He didn't elaborate when Troy gave him a questioning look. He couldn't explain why he'd agreed to the arrangement between him and Jen, and he wasn't comfortable talking about it. On the other hand, if she *did* have a baby, and Troy and Celeste knew it was his, they would be willing to feed him information.

No. He'd given Jen a promise not to interfere. He wouldn't go back on his word.

He and Troy drank their beers, lapsing into silence. It wasn't an uncomfortable silence like the one he'd felt while driving Jen home the other night. He hadn't known what to say to her. She'd made it clear she didn't welcome his questions, or his concern; acted like she was too strong to need it. That's all it was though, an act. The few times she'd let down her guard, he'd gotten glimpses of her uncertainty and vulnerability. Enough to know she needed caring for, far more than she wanted to admit. That was the real Jen, the woman he felt drawn to.

Or it could be his soft heart was messing with his hard head, which was something his brothers had often warned him about, and something he'd learned to guard more carefully than he had over the past several days.

He took another long drink and couldn't help glancing at the phone, but he didn't pick it up, and he damn sure wouldn't obsess over it anymore. He would enjoy the evening and the time he had left with Troy and Celeste. If Jen called, she could wait.

Immediately after he made that decision, his phone twanged the "Watermelon Crawl." He'd set that particular ringtone for Jen's number after seeing her dance to the song. Damn, she was a natural, and her bold little move when she backed up to him and wiggled her ass had turned him on something fierce.

Troy laughed. "Great ringtone."

The riff started over. He'd better not answer too fast, or she'd think he was desperate.

But if he waited too long, she might hang up, and he wasn't certain she would leave a voicemail. That realization had him desperately snatching up the phone. "Hey, Jen—"

"Logan! You have to get over here. Now!" Her shout damn near punctured his eardrum.

He shot to his feet. "What is it? What's wrong?"

"Come quick." She wasn't screaming anymore. Her voice trembled with anxiety, verging on panic, and made his heart pound. Whatever the hell was going on, he couldn't stand here and chat with her about it. For all he knew, she'd cut herself and was bleeding or something.

"On my way." He stuffed the cell phone into his back pocket and took off at a run, not bothering to explain anything to Troy. There wasn't time.

Logan raced around the shrubs he'd trimmed not that long ago. Her gate was open, so he let himself in the back yard and thundered across the patio to the sliding glass doors. The dog's wild barking sent a rush of adrenaline through him.

Grabbing the outside handle, he tried the door. *Locked of course.* He hammered his hand on the glass. He'd use a chair to break it if he had to.

On the other side of the door, Freckles raced back and forth, yapping like crazy, although her tail wagged, whatever that meant. She always wagged her tail, even when she sounded like she'd bite your head off.

Jen finally appeared, dressed in a big sweatshirt, bare legs, and looking a little sleepy, like she'd just woken up, or she was groggy, or...*drugged?* Shit, an overdose!

She pulled the security pin from the top of the door, then snapped open the lock.

Logan pushed the door open, rushed inside, and pulled her into his embrace. "I'm here, baby. It's all right."

His brain caught up with the wild emotion careening through him, and cautioned him to handle her with care. She could be hurt. He kept hold of her arms, in case she might be weak, while he looked her over. She didn't appear to be injured. A flushed face could mean fever.

"What's wrong?" His voice came out sharp due to his concern.

"I worked through the night, so I slept in…" Her astonished gaze fell from his face to his chest. "You…you don't have a shirt on."

He'd forgotten to grab it, and it was soaked with sweat anyway. "You told me to hurry."

The dog stopped barking and racing around in circles, and began sniffing at Logan's leg. Freckles displayed no sign of distress.

Jen's cheeks were bright, but not unnaturally rosy, and though she felt a bit warm, it wasn't enough to indicate fever. No bloody knives were lying around, no glass on the floor, nothing broken as far he could see.

"Is there some reason you called me in a panic?"

She swallowed hard before nodding.

"Do I have time to take my shoes off? They're muddy." His shorts were dirty too. But he didn't think she'd appreciate it if he shucked them along with his shoes.

She nodded and waited long enough for him to take off his sneakers and then grabbed his hand. "Come with me."

"Yes, ma'am…" He allowed her to guide him through the hallway toward the stairs. Her palm felt so smooth, incredibly soft. Was the rest of her skin like that? She wasn't willing to stop long enough for him to find out.

Logan dragged his mind back to solving the mystery that had put her in such a panic. "Is your toilet overflowing?"

"No, I didn't call you over here to fix my toilet." Her voice had a wry edge to it.

She started up the steps to the second floor. *Well, hell.* She hadn't called him over here for *no* reason. Nor could he believe she was so eager to see him, she'd phoned in a panic—after waiting three days.

He stood at the base of the stairs, mesmerized by the sight of her swaying backside, and had to run to catch up. She still hadn't explained why she'd panicked, but whatever had unnerved her wasn't life threatening.

Logan's tension drained enough for him to focus on something other than impending doom. Two large works of art on the stairway wall caught his attention. Vivid landscapes with large abstract flowers were painted on glass panes of what looked like old windows. "I like these paintings. Where'd you get them?"

"My friend is an artist. I love her work and those are my favorite pieces. She goes to estate sales, antique shops, and scours abandoned buildings to find old windows. I'm not sure how she makes the colors so vivid, unless it has something to do with how she paints on the back of the glass."

The stairs ended at a landing, which overlooked a two-story marbled entryway, lit by a wrought-iron chandelier. A loud *tick-tock* from a grandfather clock echoed in the cavernous space. "You've got a beautiful home, and a nice blend of modern and antiques."

"Eclectic."

"Right. The house I grew up in looks like the set of *Bonanza*."

"Is that what you like? Western décor?"

"Some of it, I guess. But it's not my house. If I were to build one, I'd make it different."

"How different?"

"Haven't really thought about it. I've been focused on finishing vet school. Expect I'll settle somewhere near the ranch. Details beyond that are fuzzy."

"I've had my future planned out from the time I was twelve."

"Twelve?" He released a laugh, amused, but not really surprised. "At that age, I wasn't thinking past what I wanted to eat for dinner."

She pushed open a door and he followed her into a huge bedroom. Late afternoon light shone through over-sized windows with decorative leaded glass. He barely saw what else was in the room as his gaze fixed on the bed. Blankets and sheets were thrown back, as if she was preparing to crawl in, or maybe she'd just gotten up. She'd said she slept in.

She whirled around and went for the waistband of his shorts, and already had the first two buttons undone before he managed to snap out of his shock. Good Lord, she'd lost her mind.

His hands went to hers, enveloping them and halting her frantic tearing at his buttons. "Jen, what the hell?"

She tossed dark hair out of her eyes, her hands trembling in his. "We have to do it now."

"*That's* why you called me over here like the house was on fire?"

"It's the right time. I'm ovulating, and there's a short window of opportunity."

"Okay, I get the technical stuff." He drew her to him and slipped his arms around her waist. As eager as he'd been for this, and based on how his body was reacting to her pawing, he'd have no problem *doing it* as fast as she wanted. But one look at her wild expression, and the fear in her eyes, told him she wasn't anywhere near ready. Not to mention, he smelled worse than a wet dog.

"We can afford to take a little time, you know, to set the mood. Let me wash off. I've been working in the yard. I'm sweaty and dirty."

She gripped his upper arms tight, her expression strained. "We don't have much time. Besides, this isn't about getting into the mood. I just need you to…to…*impregnate* me!"

Her blunt demand cooled the heated blood pulsing through his veins.

A stud, that's all he was to her, and he had damn sure better remember it.

"Fine, I'll do the honors, *after* I get a quick shower."

"No! No, there isn't time. We need to *do* this." She backed away from him, practically yelling. That, more than anything, told him she wasn't ready. Her way of dealing with fear was to put her head down and batter her way through the obstacle like a billy goat. If he did her bidding, it wouldn't hurt him, but it would sure as hell hurt her.

He responded in a controlled tone. "Jen, I need to be clean, and you…*you* need to calm down."

The flush on her face deepened. "I *am* calm!"

Logan laughed at the outright lie. "No, you're not. You're anxious and scared."

She crossed her arms over her chest and frowned at him. "And you're being a patronizing asshole."

"Maybe. But this 'patronizing asshole' doesn't want to hurt you. If you aren't ready for me, it *will* hurt."

She marched to the bedside table and picked up a tube. "Lubricating gel."

Of all the… Damn, if she didn't confuse him one minute and make him laugh the next. "You got this all planned out, haven't you?"

"What do *you* think?"

This was the same woman who had her life charted from the age of twelve. She probably had printed instructions on intercourse.

"I think I need a shower." He strode through the doorway that led into the master bathroom and stripped off his remaining clothes, before heading into a walk-in shower. He wasn't getting into bed with her stinking so bad he offended himself. Turning the knob, he waited until the water warmed, then stood beneath the rainfall. He found the soap and began to wash.

The shower was helping to cool him off, and he didn't rush. Their deal was that she would go to bed with him and they'd make a baby the old-fashioned way. That didn't mean *wham, bam, thank you, ma'am!*

He would take whatever enjoyment he could take, and give her as much pleasure as she'd let him. He was determined their time together, however brief, wouldn't be a bad memory for either of them.

Chapter Seven

Logan Hardt had the most amazing ass. His buttocks were muscled, slightly concave on each side, but with enough fullness to fill out his jeans. She'd followed him, angry and, yes, scared and a little bewildered, as he'd marched into her master bathroom, dropped his shorts and briefs, and strolled into her shower. The incredible sight of his bare backside rendered her speechless.

She quickly backed away from the shower's entrance, praying he hadn't seen her. Spying on him while he showered seemed so *voyeuristic*. She hadn't planned on studying him, and she didn't want him to study her. The only way she'd get through this would be to make it quick. If the foreplay dragged on, her heart would give out.

Her hand hovered at chest level before she lifted it, still shaking, to push her hair away from her face. *Now what?* She could undress and wait under the sheets and feel stupid, or she could sit on the bed and wait for him to get out of the shower, then undress and slip under the sheets. Or...she could run away, which was exactly what her body was primed to do. The level of epinephrine in her bloodstream had to be off the charts, considering her rapid heartbeat.

Logan was concerned about being sweaty. She could tell

he'd been working, but she didn't think he smelled that bad. He certainly didn't revolt her.

She lifted an arm, sniffed, but didn't smell anything. Just in case though, she grabbed a bottle of Vera Wang, pulled open the collar of her sweatshirt, and spritzed her chest. Not too much. He might start sneezing.

Oh God...what if he's allergic to perfume?

The shower went off and Jen's heart jumped. She turned in time to see Logan emerge from the shower, naked and dripping wet. She stared at his magnificent body for what seemed like, oh, at least a full minute, before he broke the trance by grabbing a towel off the rack.

She slammed her eyelids shut. Too late, his image was etched in her mind. He had the washboard abs the guys at the gym worked so hard to get, the light sprinkling of brown hair on his chest was *so* alluring.

"You can open your eyes."

She did...and honed in on the towel around his waist. He'd been semi-aroused when he walked out of the shower, and the towel bulged over his growing erection.

"Do I pass inspection?" he asked, his voice tinged with amusement.

She jerked her gaze upward and heat rushed to her face. Was that what he thought she was doing? Inspecting him? "You fit my requirements," she mumbled.

What a stupid thing to say! She walked into the bedroom before she made an even bigger fool of herself.

Holding her arms, she tried to control her trembling. If she had boots, she'd be shaking in them, but not from fear or even hyper-anxiety, this quivering had a hot urgent quality. She hadn't thought she would be so affected. Anxious? Yes. Attracted to him? Of course...but totally turned on? This was something new.

She hadn't been able, or willing, to give in to sexual attraction before, because she was so uptight around men. Even the two men she'd dated the longest. Maybe it was different with Logan, because she already knew he would be leaving; and there was a kind of freedom in not having to face him again if he ended up disappointed.

Logan's hands rested on her shoulders. She tensed, out of habit more than as a reaction to his touch, which actually didn't make her freeze up or want to run away. When he massaged the tight muscles in her shoulders and neck, she began to relax.

After a moment, he turned her to face him. His eyes met hers, but this time, there was no amusement in them. "Let's not make this about requirements. Put aside all that for a little while, and let's just be me and you, Logan and Jen, a man and woman who want each other."

"That wasn't part of the deal." She hated how her voice quavered, which made her sound more vulnerable than she felt, which was a lot, and she hadn't even taken her clothes off yet. He knew she wanted him. Except, she couldn't afford to want him, because want could be dangerous. Want could turn into need, and need could be rejected.

"Forget the deal. For now." He reached up, tucked her hair behind her ear and cupped her cheek with his palm, sending warm honey flowing through her veins.

Her fluttering pulse slowed, her breathing slowed, and soon, so did her heartbeat. Even time seemed to slow down, allowing her to focus on the moment. She put her hand over his, holding his palm against her face, not wanting to break the connection, because she was afraid the spell would end and fear would rush in.

Dipping his head, he touched her lips and she inhaled his warm breath on a gasp.

Suddenly, kissing him was all she could think about.

Eagerly, she leaned into him. He smoothed his thumb over her cheek in an affirming caress, a tender gesture that gave her courage. The defenses she'd spent half a lifetime building, began to crumble. When his arms went around her, she melted against him, sinking into his warmth and into his strength. With Logan, she felt safe, something she hadn't felt in such a long time. How ironic that she should feel so secure, despite the uncertainty of the situation.

She allowed him to pull her forward until she was pressed against him from breast to hips. He moved his hands down her back, shaping her curves, her hips and her buttocks. He touched her with confidence, like a man who knew what he wanted. She had no idea what to do next, so she would follow his lead, even though she'd never given any man that much trust, fearing what might happen. *Pain. Humiliation. Rejection.*

Logan wouldn't reject her, because she would send him away first. She'd set the ground rules, and he'd accepted them. For the first time, maybe the only time, she could put her fears aside and enjoy being with a man. *This* man.

She wound her arms around his neck and gave herself over to the kiss.

Hesitant at first, she soon grew bolder, running her hands over his shoulders, and finding his lean, corded arms endlessly fascinating. She traced her fingers over the defined muscles in his back. Touching him telegraphed pleasure to some primitive part of her brain.

When she came to where the edge of the towel wrapped his waist, she hesitated. He didn't. He dragged it out of her way and let her continue her exploration. Downward, over those firm buttocks she'd seen. Caressing his ass was even better than looking at it.

He grasped the hem of her sweatshirt and drew back just long enough to pull it over her head. She hadn't bothered to put on a bra. Instinctively, she raised her arms to cover herself.

Logan grasped her wrists and pulled her arms away, gently. "Don't hide from me."

She flushed from head to toe. Yet she couldn't stop her gaze from sliding down to his full-on erection. *Good Lord, he was huge. How would it fit...?*

He hauled her up to him, bending to kiss her again, this

time open-mouthed and demanding. Her questions and doubts, her frantic thoughts, floated away like dandelion fluff in a breeze. She could focus only on the physical sensations — the feel of his lips and tongue, where his heated skin touched hers, his arousal pressed against her stomach, hot and hard. Thinking about what he would do with it made her a little dizzy.

She couldn't let her mind go there yet, or she would invite fear back into the mix, and she was enjoying this pleasurable prelude. Now wasn't the time for insecurity and uncertainty. That would come later, and with it, the gnawing emotional hunger that seemed impossible to satisfy. Logan couldn't fix her, he couldn't fill the emptiness, but his touch could make it go away for a little while.

He continued to kiss her as he moved them both to the bed, pressing her down onto the rumpled sheets, pausing long enough to hook her lacy panties with his fingers and tug them off. Then he moved over her, rising up to trail kisses from the side of her mouth, along her jawline, and down her neck. He traced her collarbone with his lips. All the while, his hands skimmed her body, *worshiping*. That was the only word she could come up with to describe how he touched her.

She wasn't sure if she should try to kiss him while he was kissing her, or just lay back and enjoy it. He'd taken the lead though, so she would let him guide her. He clearly knew what he was doing.

He moved lower, stroking his hand up her side to her breast, cradling the soft flesh, while he used his lips to explore. His thumb brushed a sensitive nipple, before gently capturing it with his teeth.

She gasped, her thoughts scattering.

He alternated between sucking and licking and using his teeth, gently abrading the increasingly sensitized nub. Jen squirmed, unable to hold back a moan, as pleasure rippled out in all directions.

Moving to the other breast, he gave it the same

treatment, using just the right combination of gentleness and roughness to bring her exquisite pleasure.

"You're beautiful, Jen..." His warm breath bathed her skin, setting off new quivers.

Beautiful? She couldn't see the beauty in herself. Yet he made her *feel* beautiful, and sensual, and desirable.

He blazed a trail down her stomach, stopping to circle her belly button with his tongue, before moving lower. He whispered for her to open her legs. She did, after a brief hesitation. Exposed to him in this way, which was so much more intimate than anything she'd ever experienced, was terrifying and exhilarating, all at the same time.

When he nuzzled the apex of her thighs and put his lips on her, she felt like she would burst into flames and melt beneath the heat. All sense of feeling, all sensation, constricted to one small spot that throbbed and ached, the same spot he licked. The pleasure-pain grew so intense she could hardly catch her breath.

Jen ignored the warnings going off in her head telling her she needed to get away. Her body wouldn't let her. It wanted to move closer and wasn't obeying her fear at the moment.

With only his lips and tongue, Logan stripped away her inhibitions. He ratcheted up her arousal until all she cared about was what he could do to her with his mouth and tongue. Arching her hips, she tried to move to meet each stroke, but he held her in place and wouldn't let her hurry. He controlled the timing and the pressure. He backed off when she wanted him to go faster, then pressed in and drove her to a precipice, not letting up until her legs grew weak and fell open to give him greater access.

He let go of her hip, and then his fingers were inside her, deep and thrusting, while he continued to torment her with his tongue. Gasping, she dug her heels into the bed. The sensations built and built until she couldn't catch her breath. She fought to hold back, fearing if she let go, she would break into a million pieces. She was stripped and bared in a way that had little to do with being naked, and she couldn't prevent what was about to happen.

The shuddering tremor set off an earthquake that ripped through her body, tearing her asunder in a terrible, wonderful, indescribable coming apart—her own personal "big bang." The resulting waves swelled and crashed over her. When her soul finally rejoined her body, she felt different. Her life had been remade into something that was so much more than the dry, colorless existence she'd been leading.

Logan gave her little time to marvel at the miracle. After kissing the inside of her thighs, he made his way up her body, trailing more kisses over her belly and breasts. He came up over her, braced on his arms, and pressed a moist kiss on her parted lips, while at the same time lowering his body. A thick blunt force pressed against her slick wet opening. As he slid inside, the pressure increased, along with the sensation of being stretched, and filled to capacity.

Too much, this was too much! He was too much! She couldn't contain him. Mostly, she couldn't contain the groundswell of emotion.

He nuzzled her ear, whispering, "Relax," before he buried himself all the way to the hilt.

She gasped, and with an instinctive reflex, sank her nails into the back of his shoulders. He didn't seem to notice, or didn't care. Instead of pushing him away, she pulled him closer. Self-preservation demanded retreat, but she was powerless to do anything except surrender.

When he began to move, she considered telling him to stop, but not because he was hurting her. The brief flash of pain had passed, and she was becoming accustomed to the sense of fullness, and actually starting to like it, which made her predicament even worse. With a moan, she rose up to meet him. In response, he flexed his hips. His hard body rubbed against her sensitive flesh, sending a shower of pleasure cascading over her.

Oh, that felt good. More than good, it felt right.

Logan reached down, cupping her butt cheeks, and hauled her up against him. With every thrust, he drove in deeper, driving in the pleasure, forcing her to take more, until his thrusts pounded through every part of her. He was pushing her to a second peak, another total surrender. Letting him destroy and remake her once was dangerous enough, allowing him to repeat it would be downright stupid. But he was inside her, and around her, and he overwhelmed her senses, she could smell only him, taste only him. How could she prevent a bond being forged when he was so much a part of her?

She cried out for mercy. "Logan…please…"

He kissed her ear. "I've got you, sugar," he rasped. "I won't let go."

Drowning, she clung to him. He was firm and unmovable, like a large boulder in a raging river. If she held on, she could survive the flood. She hadn't imagined it would be like this when she'd agreed to sleep with him. What a soft, insipid metaphor for something so large and powerful. This wasn't sleeping, and it wasn't even pure sex, it was intimacy, possession, two things she had run from for years.

He ground his hips against her, giving her bursts of pleasure that made her gasp. With every thrust, an incoming tide of emotion surged through her. She sensed what he gave her could fill the void, but with something that was equally frightening. Yet she needed it more than she'd needed anything in her whole life.

She let her head fall back. He feasted on her throat as she ran her hands over his chest, stroking him and discovering, to her delight, that his flat nipples were sensitive too. His breathing became ragged, harsh, with short catches in between groans of pleasure. His thrusts came faster, harder. A sense of power rushed through her as control shifted. Or maybe she wasn't in control at all and they were hurtling, blind, into uncharted territory. She didn't care anymore. Nothing mattered but finding the intense satisfaction only Logan could give her.

Holding him tight, she entangled him with her legs and urged him on as he drove harder, higher, taking them to the very top of the roller coaster. With a low growl, he grabbed her face between his hands and gave her a fierce, desperate kiss.

Jen shuddered as they reached the peak, teetered, on the edge of oblivion, and then she fell, crying out, yet unafraid, safe in his arms.

Logan's thrusts increased in speed and urgency. He stiffened, and then groaned as his release pumped out of him. His chest heaved until at last, he dropped his head, and his ragged breath heated her neck. He'd held himself up during their lovemaking, careful not to rest his full weight on her, but now his arms collapsed.

She cradled him close, welcoming the heaviness; knowing, in that moment, he belonged to her as no one ever had, or ever would again. Tears leaked from the corners of her eyes and slid down her temples, as she ran her hands over his sweat-slicked skin. He'd been worried about his sweat offending her. Nothing about him offended her.

He'd given her something precious…and he'd given her a child. Somehow she knew this, deep inside, and she was glad he'd talked her into doing it this way. He'd given her a memory to treasure, a memory that would bring her tears, but also would comfort her when she was feeling lonely and unlovable.

After another moment, he propped himself up on his elbows. His lips curled into the sexiest smile she'd ever seen, and he regarded her with a hooded look. Reflected in his gaze was utter satisfaction and, oh God…*tenderness*.

Something shifted inside her chest, as another emotional tidal wave took her breath away. Without thinking, she framed his face with her hands and drew him down so she could kiss him. She wanted to remember everything: the way he felt inside her, the weight of his body, his slick skin, how soft and pliant his lips were. She needed to memorize his smell, his flavor, gorge on every sensation, every single thing about him, because that would be all she had left after he was gone.

Regret clogged her throat, so thick she feared she would choke on it. But there was no looking back, and no second-guessing her decision. As easily as he'd torn down her defenses, it wouldn't be long before he saw in her what others had seen, and he would leave anyway. If she tried to hold on, she'd lose him. Better to let him go. At least then, it would be her choice.

Jen abruptly broke off the kiss and pushed on his shoulders. "Time to go, cowboy."

Logan didn't move. He was too stunned, besides being worn out. His release had been nothing short of explosive, unlike anything he'd ever experienced. Maybe it had something to do with not using a condom. He'd felt every sensation so much better, her slick muscles contracting around him, milking his seed, stealing his soul... If she sent him away, she'd have to give that back.

He nuzzled her neck. She smelled of sex. Oh, yeah, he'd satisfied her, and she'd more than satisfied him, and as soon as he could rouse himself, they'd do it again.

"Come on, Logan. We're done. You need to leave." Her voice had a weird dull quality, which sent a quiver of unease through him. After the third time she shoved him, he finally rolled off her, but then he reached for her, having a strong desire to cuddle, something he didn't normally do after having sex. This time though, was different. In fact, *everything* about this was different.

Jen rolled away from him, pulled the covers over her head and curled into a ball with her back to him. She couldn't mean for him to leave right now, not after that mind-blowing bout of sex. No, not just sex; there was more to it than that, a hell of lot more. He knew it and, more importantly, *she* knew it. That's why she was throwing him out. She couldn't handle what just happened. For that matter, he wasn't sure he could either.

He braced his hands on the bed, and turned to stare, once again, in disbelief, at the lump under the sheets. Jen had come apart in his arms not once, but twice. Then, while they'd still been buzzed on an orgasmic high, she'd kissed him like he was air and she needed him in order to breathe. Her sudden rejection left him dazed, more than a little confused, and with a dull ache in his chest.

"Sure you don't want to go another round? You're paying enough for it." He'd tried for sarcasm, but his voice came out rough and made him sound desperate.

She burrowed deeper under the covers.

The longer he sat there, the worse it would be. She'd start to pity him.

He walked unevenly into the bathroom to collect his clothes, paused when he passed the towel on the floor, and remembered how she had stared at him when he'd emerged from the shower. He'd never gotten so hard so fast. She'd acted matter-of-fact about having sex with him, and it pissed him off, but then, when he'd gotten her into bed, all he could think about was satisfying her.

She hadn't acted like a woman who knew all about pleasing a man, her reactions had seemed to surprise her. But once he'd gotten past her momentary hesitance, she'd given herself to him without reservation, with more passion than he'd imagined.

Before, she'd been under his skin, an itch that wouldn't go away. Now, she was in his blood. He had to purge this ridiculous fascination. She'd gotten what she wanted; he'd gotten what he wanted. The truth was, he'd gotten *more* than he wanted; expecting her to be a quick, forgettable lay was akin to expecting a cougar to be a kitten.

After buttoning his shorts, he twisted to look at the scratches on the back of his shoulder. She'd marked him with her claws, and not just his skin. He was stupid for letting this get emotional, considering she'd made it clear from the start that all she wanted was something physical. Even less, physiological.

On his way to the bedroom door, Logan passed by the bed, where Jen still lay curled up, unmoving. She'd looked like she'd wanted to curl up in a ball the other night when they'd gone to the bar and she'd panicked. He suspected more than crowds bothered her. Maybe some asshole had wounded her, or there was some other reason she was so afraid to let him get close. He'd busted down her defenses, and now she was trying to rebuild them. If he walked out, he might never know why.

Did it matter? He was leaving, just as they'd agreed.

Damn it! He couldn't just leave without knowing she'd be all right.

He circled to her side of the bed, where she had the coverlet pulled up past her eyes, and only the dark crown of her head was visible. Hiding, just as he suspected. He longed to rip the covers off. She shouldn't hide from him. Not after what they'd done, and what she'd given him...what he had tried to give her. Somewhere along the way, he'd begun to care for her, and he'd gotten the idea into his head she might care for him. Getting involved with a woman hadn't been on his agenda for this trip, but he couldn't just walk away. To hell with their deal, this wasn't some business arrangement, even if she thought she could make it one.

The mattress sank as he sat down and reached out to pull away her covers, but then changed his mind. Jen didn't react well to being cornered. Instead of exposing her, he'd draw her out of her shell slowly. He placed his hand on the rounded area that he deduced was her shoulder.

"You okay?"

"Fine," came her muffled response. Her voice sounded strained, and even cracked a little at the end, like she was crying.

The hard thudding in his chest turned into a ferocious

ache. Yeah, he'd given her something all right...*pain*. She was so small and tight, which he'd assumed meant she was nervous. But the moment he sank inside her, he couldn't stop. He didn't recall her reacting as if it hurt, but he hadn't been thinking very clearly at that point.

"Did I hurt you?"

She shook her head.

"Will you come out from under the covers and look at me, so I'll believe you?"

Her fingers appeared over the edge of the covers, and after a few moments hesitation, she drew them downward until just her eyes showed, the color reminding him of fallen leaves. They grew round — bright with tears, and filled with regret. He wasn't ready for that, and the impact slammed into him like an unexpected punch.

"I'm not hurt," she murmured.

"Then why do you have that wounded deer look in your eyes?"

She lowered her lashes, shielding her gaze from him. After a moment, she reached out to where his hand rested on the covers, laid her palm over his knuckles and curled her fingers, holding his hand. Maybe she meant to reassure him, but her gentle touch acted like a lash on his heart. He stared at her narrow palm and the long elegant fingers and slender wrist. She was small-boned, fragile, and he'd plowed into her with less care than a bull mounting a cow.

"You didn't hurt me, Logan. I got used to it, once I got over the surprise."

"The surprise?" Had she expected him to be smaller? Nothing about him indicated small.

"I wasn't sure what to expect. I've never done that before."

He jerked his gaze to her face, finding breathing difficult. No, she could be...he would've realized...he should've *noticed*. "What do you mean, 'never done that? Never, as in *never*?"

The covers dropped lower, revealing a sad smile. She

used the edge of the sheet to wipe tears from her eyes. "Unbelievable, isn't it, a thirty-year-old virgin? I'm surprised you didn't realize, considering I had no idea what I was doing. I have watched a few movies though."

"You might've warned me." He thrust his fingers through his hair, mostly annoyed with himself for not picking up on the obvious clues. "I would've slowed down. Been more careful."

"I didn't want you to be careful. I wanted exactly what you gave me."

He was almost afraid to ask. "What was that?"

"Pleasure, an experience I'll remember forever, and hopefully, a baby."

The knot in his stomach tightened as she pushed him back into the tidy box she'd created for him.

"Well that was the plan." His reply came out sounding bitter, but he was tired of pretending to be all right with this arrangement.

"Why are you angry?" She had to gall to look perplexed. Where did he start? Trying to explain wouldn't make any difference, not unless she changed her mind about seeing him again, which he didn't expect she would. But he wasn't leaving without some answers.

"Why are *you* afraid?"

She blinked as if he'd slapped her. "I don't know what you're talking about."

"Sure you do. You won't let me stay and hold you because you're terrified you might like it."

She gathered the sheets to her chest. "You don't know anything about me."

He released a frustrated huff. "You're right, I don't, because you won't tell me anything."

"There's nothing to tell."

"The hell there isn't, you still haven't told me why you're so set on raising a baby alone."

"I *did* tell you. I haven't met anyone."

"Bullshit. You're beautiful and smart; I can't believe

you haven't met a thousand guys who want to date you."

"I didn't want to date them."

"Why not? Is no one good enough?"

She glared at him. *Good!* Her anger was easier to deal with than her vulnerability. "That has nothing to do with it. I'm just not comfortable with…intimacy."

"You were comfortable enough a little while ago."

Her blush told him he'd hit on the truth. "Because you're—"

"Because I'm what?" Finally, he just might get some idea of how she felt about him, other than for stud service.

"Because you're *leaving,* and I don't have to see you again, so I don't have to worry about when you'll decide you don't want me anymore."

He had to process her weird explanation before it made any sense, and when it finally did somehow make sense, it made him angry. "Oh, I see. You're okay with *physical* intimacy, so long as you don't have to commit or risk anything, and you need to blame somebody else for your fear of abandonment or rejection, or whatever it is."

With a scowl, she pushed up into a sitting position, still holding the covers, and tucked the sheets under her arms. He thought about telling her it was too late, he'd already seen — and handled — the goods.

"Don't psychoanalyze me. You aren't qualified, and I didn't invite it."

"Maybe you should consider seeing someone who *is* qualified!" The instant he blurted the thoughtless retort, he wanted to retract it.

Hurt flashed in her eyes, before her face froze into a hard mask. "You need to leave. We're done."

Damn it, she was rejecting him first so he wouldn't have a chance to reject her. He knew that's what she was doing, but knowing something logically didn't mean it hurt any less.

He shouldn't have agreed to this ridiculous deal, or he should've backed out after realizing he could care for her.

She was right about one thing, though. He couldn't fix whatever was wrong. She wasn't even willing to lean on him, or to consider the possibility that she could depend on someone other than herself. She ought to get to know him better, before deciding he was like whoever had hurt her and made her doubt herself and everyone else. But that still might not change her mind, and he was on a direct course for getting his heart broken if he kept this up much longer.

Besides, he was leaving on Sunday.

Logan stood. He'd given her what she wanted. What more was there to discuss? "Yes, ma'am. I'll show myself out."

Chapter Eight

Logan slowed his truck as he followed the signs directing him to the arriving flights at the airport terminal and concentrated on dodging pedestrians. The chaos that emerged from the doors of the terminal as passengers poured out reaffirmed his decision to drive to Atlanta, so he hadn't had to go through all that. He'd decided he'd come out early to spend some time with Troy before the big day, but his brother, Huston, who'd also known Troy since they were kids, had only been able to come out for the weekend. Fortunately, his brother didn't appear to mind dealing with all the things involved with traveling by air.

Spotting his brother, which wasn't difficult, as Huston was the only man wearing a black Stetson. He was standing outside near a spot where other cars were picking up travelers, holding an Army-issued duffel bag, and wearing a shit-eating grin. His stance, with one hip cocked to the side, looked slightly off-kilter.

Guilt ate at Logan. If he'd accompanied his brother into the Army, instead of going to college, he might've somehow prevented the disaster that had taken Huston's leg and their friend's life.

Huston tossed his bag in the truck bed, then opened the door and dipped into the cab, pausing to adjust his right leg before he could swing in his left one. The jeans he wore were special-made to fit over a prosthetic knee, and his custom-made cowboy boots had a zipper up the side so they'd fit over the false foot. More than his choice in clothing had changed as the result of a single explosion, yet Huston refused to talk about his time in Afghanistan, which bothered Logan to no end, because they'd shared everything. Off-limits meant unresolved. Before the weekend was over, he would urge Huston to go back to the psychiatrist. If he didn't trust the one from the VA, he could find another.

"You're late," Huston said, before he punched Logan on the shoulder.

"Blame the traffic. Took me an hour to drive ten miles. You're lucky I made it before you turned gray." Logan pulled up behind a red bus and waited his turn to get the hell out of there.

His brother snapped the seatbelt. "You know Hardts don't turn gray before they're sixty."

"Dad's fifty-six and has more than a few gray hairs."

"Those are ones *you've* given him." Huston enjoyed his joke, but he knew he'd been the one who put gray hairs on both their parents' heads with his daredevil antics. Though as far as Logan knew, his brother had never impregnated a woman under contract.

"How is the old man, by the way?"

"I left Jake strict instructions not to get him riled." Huston placed his hat on the front seat and smoothed his fingers over coal-black hair, the color shared by two other brothers and their father.

"You left instructions? For *Jake*?" Logan released a disbelieving laugh. No one could tell Jake anything. Their older brother already knew it all.

"He's come down a few pegs since Alison left." Huston had his head turned, and was looking out the window at the traffic so Logan couldn't see his face, but he didn't need to see Huston's expression to know his brother wasn't kidding around anymore. Jake's wife had filed for a divorce after accusing him of cheating on her. He swore it wasn't true. Logan had stayed out of it. He wasn't about to step into that rattlesnake nest. He had enough problems of his own to deal with, what to do about Jen being the biggest.

Huston slumped in the seat and popped a piece of gum into his mouth. He'd gained a little weight and looked like he might've started working out again, but was still thinner than when he'd left home to go into the service. He was thirteen months Logan's senior, but they'd always looked the same age. Now though, Huston definitely appeared older. Stress had deepened the brackets around his mouth, and the dark circles beneath his eyes seemed to indicate he didn't get enough sleep. His bouts of depression worried Logan, but he didn't know what to do about it, other than encourage his brother to see a shrink, which Huston continued to resist.

He offered Logan a piece of gum. "How did things turn out with your gal?"

"She's not my gal." *Far from it.* Logan watched the signs carefully, since he didn't trust the map lady on his phone. He hadn't thought Jen would cause him to become lost either, but here he was, groping his way through the kind of heartbreak he'd sworn to avoid. How had he fallen so fast, and for a woman who'd made her expectations crystal clear? Maybe he ought to have *his* head examined.

He nearly missed the entrance to the freeway thanks to Jen...or thanks to his inability to not think about her for more than a few moments so he could pay attention. Throwing a quick look over his shoulder to check his blind spot, he sped up and veered over two lanes, swerving onto the ramp at the last moment.

Huston shook his head. "You drive like an old man. Somebody's gonna run over your ass one day."

"I haven't gotten a ticket."

"That's only because the cops won't stop a car they can catch on foot."

"Are you practicing for a new career as a comedian?"

"Think I could make it?"

"If you were funny." Logan moved to the middle lane and pressed the accelerator until he'd reached seventy, five miles over the speed limit. He didn't tear down the highway, nor did he seek adventures and take huge risks, like his brothers did. He preferred to move slowly, and generally he stayed on course. He hadn't done either of those things though, after he'd met Jen.

"So did you sleep with her?"

Not surprisingly, his brother went back to the subject Logan most wanted to avoid. In the past, they'd always talked about their relationships pretty freely. This time however, he wasn't comfortable gossiping about what he'd done with Jen. What they had shared was between the two of them. "It's none of your business."

Huston's eager expression fell. "Ah hell, Logan. *I* don't get any. At least tell me about what *you're* getting."

"I'm not getting anything. Not anymore. That's all there is to tell."

Gaining Huston's undivided attention wasn't Logan's intent, but he had it now anyway, although Huston's smile had all but vanished. "Did she really pay you to screw her?"

Logan frowned. He hadn't asked for the money she'd promised, and had already decided he wouldn't. He shouldn't have agreed to her deal in the first place. "She offered to pay me to be a sperm donor. I was the one who put conditions on it and got her into bed. I don't know if I got her pregnant. Don't care."

Silence was worse than the wisecracks. Huston knew he was lying.

"You didn't do anything she didn't want," he said finally. Being a good brother, he'd offered a helpful excuse.

"That's what I keep telling myself. But she..." Logan searched for the right words. "She's been hurt. Something, or somebody, messed her up bad, and I'm not sure I didn't make it worse."

Logan slammed on the brakes as traffic came to a halt, which was one more thing he hated about big cities. He also hated how he'd left Jen. They'd hit a roadblock, he'd gotten angry, and now he regretted some of things he'd said. Even so, he would honor her request and stay away. If she wanted to talk to him, she knew where to find him.

"She's a grown woman, right? You aren't responsible for her."

The cars in front of them began to move again, and Logan was tempted to open the door and push Huston out before he drove off. So what if he had an overdeveloped protective streak? He'd bedded a virgin, possibly gotten her pregnant. How the hell could he *not* feel responsible?

"She won't *let* me be responsible, so don't worry about it."

He'd been blessed, or cursed, with a sixth sense when it came to women, which was why so many of them confided in him—except for Jen. She hadn't confided shit. He knew though, deep down, she needed him. At the same time, she was the least needy woman he knew. Successful, wealthy, smart and capable, the only obvious thing she lacked was someone to share her life with. For some reason, she flat refused to entertain the possibility that person might be him. Of course, he was in no position to take on a family and had little to offer her anyway. The fact he'd even entertained the possibility ought to scare him to death.

Logan tightened his fingers around the steering wheel. He couldn't talk about this anymore. "Has dad decided whether he'll sell the west section?" Like his father, he was loath to part with land, but selling off property would put some much-needed cash in the bank, and he would feel less guilty about going back to school.

"You know we can't sell to anyone except Hardt descendants," Huston replied, gazing straight ahead, but seeming to look far away. "Only old Buck can afford to buy our land, and Miss Kate won't let him have one foot, much less a whole section."

Logan was familiar with the stipulation, which had existed since the first Hardt divided his land among his children, five generations back. The descendants had lived alongside each other peacefully, until something had happened between his grandfather and a distant cousin, setting off a lifetime feud. They'd have to find some other way to improve the bottom line. His schooling would have to wait.

Huston propped his arm on the open window frame and seemed focused on the passing scenery. "Was it worth it?"

Logan sure was glad his brother wasn't looking at him. Otherwise, Huston might've seen him swallow tears. He would've never lived *that* down. His brother's quiet question wasn't a joke, and wasn't meant to rile him. He didn't have to respond, but he owed it to himself to consider the answer.

Had screwing Jen been worth it? That wasn't even the right term. He wasn't sure what to call it, but it wasn't run-of-the-mill screwing. He'd left a part of himself behind, and still didn't know how it had happened. He'd never felt...*whatever* it was he felt.

His parents had met at a rodeo and, according to them, had fallen head-over-heels on the first date. Was that what happened to him? At one time, he'd wanted to experience the kind of love his folks had shared, but that didn't work so well when only one person was willing. He doubted he'd see Jen again, but it didn't stop him from hoping he would.

"Yeah," he said finally. "She's worth it."

Huston turned his head, his expression dead serious. "Does she think you're worth it?"

Chapter Nine

A wedding was about to take place in the back yard of the house next to Jen's. Troy and Celeste had invited her and she had RSVP'd. Not showing up would make it look like she was avoiding Logan, —or staying home and licking her wounds because he was avoiding her.

Since she'd sent him away, he hadn't returned. He hadn't so much as shown his face. She'd gone out to the backyard every morning and again when she got home in the evenings, doing her exercises and playing with Freckles, all in hopes Logan might happen to be outside next door. She would see him over the trimmed bushes and she would wave, and maybe, he'd come over and she would apologize for being a jerk.

This morning, the caterers and florist had been busy setting up tables and decorating a new arbor in her neighbor's yard. She'd seen Troy and Celeste, two older couples who might be their parents, and several younger people who could be siblings or friends. But she hadn't seen Logan.

She turned in front of a full-length mirror in her dressing room. Having changed half a dozen times, she'd finally opted for a little black dress that was her go-to outfit when she needed something classy, a dress that looked like one Audrey Hepburn had worn.

Jen smoothed her hands over the fitted skirt. Regular exercise kept her slender, though not nearly as slim as Audrey Hepburn. Still, the dress complemented her figure. She hoped Logan might notice. That is, if he took notice of her at all. After the way they'd parted he might never look at her again, much less speak to her. He had the right to hate her, given the way she'd treated him.

The ache in her chest that had started the moment he walked out the door hadn't gotten better, but ached even more, like a bruise she kept re-injuring. The throbbing started up again every time she thought about him, which was about a hundred times a day. Even Freckles had become listless. The poor dog stood in front of the sliding glass doors, her tail slowly moving, back and forth. Watching. Waiting.

Jen stooped to scratch behind the dog's ears. "I'm sorry, sweetie. He's not coming back—" She fought tears.

The dog's brown-eyed gaze rebuked her.

"Don't look at me like that. It wouldn't have worked out." So Jen had been telling herself for three days, but she still wasn't convinced. In fact, the more she thought about it, the more she feared she'd totally screwed up her one chance at happiness.

Regardless, she had to stop hiding. She would go to the wedding and if Logan gave her a chance to apologize, maybe they could work something out. It was a long shot, and a big "if" and "maybe," but she had to try.

Just beyond entrance to her back yard, a worn path led through an opening in the evergreen bushes. She wondered about the people who had once lived in her home and the ones who'd lived next door when the hedges were first planted. They must have been close friends, which would explain the path.

Troy and Celeste were little more than strangers to her, and she suspected they'd only invited her to the wedding because she lived next door. She had to do a better job of being a good neighbor. In New York, no one much cared, but down here, being neighborly was a prerequisite for ensuring acceptance. Most of her life, she'd been something of a loner. She didn't want her child to grow up like that. She couldn't imagine Logan without friends. He could draw people to him like a bright flower drew butterflies.

Her anxiety ratcheted up when she passed through a wrought iron gate into her neighbor's back yard. She made a quick survey of her surroundings, as always, to make sure she knew where all the exits were. There weren't as many people as she thought there would be; maybe fifty, and most of them were seated in rows of wooden folding chairs. The yard was big enough that they wouldn't be crowded together after the ceremony.

Glowing lanterns hung in the trees, providing soft light for a celebration that would last into the evening. Ivy wrapped handrails along a stone walkway and twined through an arbor next to a fishpond. The air smelled like freshly mowed grass and faintly of magnolias, which bloomed in trees around the yard. A spraying fountain added a natural ambiance to the strains of a string quartet playing Mozart. If she were to marry, she would want a wedding like this one, outdoors, in a place where she was comfortable.

She didn't see Logan, but knew he'd be with the wedding party. The men in black tuxes, including the one approaching her, were ushers.

"Ma'am, may I escort you to a seat?" The dark-haired man, who offered her his arm, had a friendly smile and a distinct Texas accent. Her neighbor, Troy, hailed from the Lone Star State, so this must be one of his friends or relatives.

"Yes, please." Jen took the usher's arm. He wasn't quite as tall as Logan, but had a similar rangy build, although he was leaner, to the point of being too thin. He didn't swagger when he walked, like Logan did. In fact, he seemed to be favoring his right leg. Something about him looked vaguely familiar, yet she knew she'd never met him. "Are you here from Texas?"

"How could you tell?" His eyes, which looked closer to gray or green than blue, gleamed with amusement. "You must be the pretty neighbor."

His assessment? Or something he'd heard?

"Is there an ugly one?" she retorted.

"If there is, I haven't met her. Do you have any stepsisters?"

Quick-witted *and* good looking, and not wearing a wedding band... *Girls, look out!*

"No cruel step-sisters, no glass slippers either, and I decided against the frothy gown."

"If you're worried your prince will be disappointed, don't be." Her escort's sly smile implied some private joke. She couldn't see Logan bragging about her to his friends, or if he had, she doubted he'd have presented her in a very positive light. He'd left angry and had stayed away. She could only assume that meant he wanted nothing more to do with her, which was her own fault entirely. The knot of misery in her chest moved up into her throat.

The usher stopped at a seat at the end of a row, two-thirds of the way back. Had she given him instructions, she couldn't have picked a better spot. She'd be able see everything, but if need be, could escape without attracting attention.

She smiled as she let go of his arm. "Thank you. This is perfect."

He gave a nod. "Enjoy the evening, Cinderella."

Cute. He'd suggested she would turn into a pumpkin at some point, or maybe he'd implied she would meet up with her prince. If so, Logan might throw the glass slipper at her.

Who *was* that usher? She turned, but he was too far away to call back. She should've gotten his name. He hadn't asked for hers, though it seemed he might already know it. She felt at a distinct disadvantage.

Within moments, the music changed, and the minister took his place with four other men, who joined him near the arbor.

Jen's heart fluttered the moment she spotted Logan next to the groom. He stood several inches taller than the other men. The late afternoon light reflected off his blond-streaked hair, and she noticed he'd gotten it cut short. She wished he'd left it long and curling over his collar. She loved running her fingers through the thick strands. He hadn't asked for her opinion however, and she wouldn't be touching his hair again at any rate. Regardless of the haircut, he was by far the handsomest man up there. The fawn-colored tux complimented his sun-streaked hair. He looked as fabulous in formal wear as he did in faded jeans and t-shirts.

He looked even more fabulous stark naked.

Her pulse accelerated. He hadn't seen her yet, or maybe he wasn't even looking for her. She held him in her gaze, hoping she might catch his eye at some point. After the wedding, sometime during the reception, hopefully when so many people weren't around, she would approach him and ask if he would come over to say goodbye before he left. That would give her a chance to talk to him in private.

The music swelled and the bridal party began their procession. Attendants in taupe, floor-length dresses swished past. Each carried a leafy bouquet with a creamy floral mix. The soothing neutrals suited the outdoorsy setting.

Jen stood with the others as the music shifted and the bride appeared.

Celeste's strapless champagne gown, with its loose flowing skirt, was simple, yet stunning. She wore her curly light-brown hair loose, adorned with a small spray of leafy white flowers that someone had expertly fastened behind one ear to make the effect look casual, like she'd been out in a field gathering wildflowers. She glowed as she made her way to the grinning groom.

Tears blurred Jen's vision. She blinked and dabbed a

tissue in the corner of her eyes to avoid smearing her makeup. She might never know that kind of happiness. Worse, she might've thrown away her only opportunity. Except for the fact that Logan was leaving. Even if she could change the way they'd parted, she couldn't change the future. Their lives had intersected at the wrong time. He had a dream; she had a career. That was all there was to it.

After the ceremony, she made her way to one of the tables and waited.

"It was a beautiful wedding," gushed an older woman.

"Yes, it was," Jen acknowledged, and smiled. She wasn't in the mood to talk, but she forced herself to make polite conversation with the people seated around her. Her flagging hope sank lower when Logan never once ventured her direction.

The wedding party had congregated at a far table. He'd noticed her, or she thought he had. She could get up and go over there, congratulate the bride and groom, greet Logan, and open the door for further conversation. That meant passing through the crowd and risking rejection if he responded with cool politeness.

Her watch vibrated. The phone call she'd scheduled with the agency team was coming up in half an hour.

Pull it together. Get up and go talk to him. Get his attention before—

"Can I have everyone's attention?"

She jerked her head up at the sound of Logan's voice.

He came to his feet, champagne glass in hand, and held it high to make a toast. She hoped it would be a short one. If she didn't get a chance to talk to him tonight, she might not see him before he left.

"As Troy's best man, I have the honor of making a toast. Oh boy, have I been waiting for this! A chance to tell everyone the truth—"

"Careful now." Troy leaned back and put his arm around Celeste, who gave him a questioning look. She appeared more worried about the truth than he did.

Logan's smile broadened. "I've known Troy for what seems like forever. Our mothers were best friends. We went through school together, through Boy Scouts, played football, double-dated…" He leaned near the couple. "Just so you know, Celeste, he didn't have good taste in women until he met you."

"That *is* the truth," Troy said, laughing.

Logan straightened, still addressing the newlyweds. "I've got to admit, I was surprised when Troy told me he was moving to Georgia. Didn't reckon anything could drag him out of Texas, not even a sweet gal. But when I met you, Celeste, I figured out the reason for Troy's defection. He's found his best friend."

Logan's expression grew serious. "I've heard people talk about being friends and lovers. But I thought that's all it is, only talk. Most relationships aren't strong enough to hold on through all the crap life throws at you. My mom and dad were the only couple I knew who had that kind of bond…until I came out here and saw how the two of you are with each other. Better together."

His wry smile appeared, showing off hid adorable dimple, which was more visible when he was clean-shaven. "Actually, I don't know if Troy improved you any, Celeste, but you sure did make this cowboy a better man."

Troy lifted his glass. "That's the truth."

Celeste beamed.

Jen swallowed the thickness in her throat. What a lucky couple to have found each other, and how lucky Logan had been to have parents who modeled true love. She couldn't say whether or not her parents had, at one time, made each other better. If so, it would've been before she came along.

Logan looked out over the crowd and his gaze fastened on hers, sending a jolt straight through her. "That's what a marriage should be…a joining of friends, who hold each other's hearts gently, with love and trust."

Jen released a shuddering breath. He'd meant that last bit for her. Troy and Celeste already understood what a good marriage was all about, and so did Logan. She was the one who didn't get it. Now she did, and it confirmed what she already knew—a good marriage was something she would never have.

She couldn't offer anyone her complete trust, not even Logan. He wouldn't accept anything less, and he deserved that kind of relationship. What was the point in talking to him and trying to mend the breach? The best thing for both of them would be to let him go.

Jen waited until the toasts were over, then bid those at her table goodbye. She'd come back later to congratulate Troy and Celeste. She couldn't stay here another minute without breaking down.

Logan swore under his breath when Jen bolted. He hadn't been able to get away to talk to her, and he'd directed most of his remarks to the happy couple, but he'd made eye contact with her when he said that last part, wanting her to hear his promise. He'd offered her friendship, which he suspected would deepen into love if she would only give this thing between them a chance.

Frankly, he'd wondered whether she would even show up, because it meant she would have to deal with the crowd — and him. Seeing her arrive was the first hopeful sign since she'd kicked him out. After two days of agonizing over whether he'd done the right thing by keeping his distance, he wasn't letting her run away.

He set his glass on the table and leaned down to Troy. "Be back in a sec. Need to straighten something out."

"Take your time. We're doin' good here." He kissed Celeste. "Aren't we, sugar?"

"*Whooie!* This is getting too sweet for me." Huston draped an arm around Logan's shoulders and raised the beer bottle in his hand. "Nice speech, little brother. You might've gone on too long; the clock struck midnight and your princess ran away."

Already annoyed by Jen's departure, Logan was in no mood for Huston's needling. He shrugged off his brother's arm. "*Little* brother? I'm three inches taller than you, and since when did you start watching Disney movies?"

Huston's eyes rounded with a look of feigned surprise. "You forgot all those movies Miss Kate made us watch?"

Their grandmother had started a tradition of movie nights when they were young. Everyone got a chance to pick one, even her. She always wanted Disney movies, usually the ones involving princesses, which surprised the boys, because she wasn't the princess type.

"Yeah, I remember. But I didn't memorize them."

"Maybe you should have."

Logan strode away, his brother's laughter following him. Huston had been cracking jokes about him and Jen ever since arriving. He'd warned Huston to mind his manners when he went to seat her, and told him where she should sit, just in case she needed to step away for some fresh air. He hadn't anticipated she would flee before he got a chance to talk to her. It would be his luck that his brother had scared her off with some crazy story.

He slipped through the same narrow path in the hedges she'd taken just moments before. With luck, he could meet her at the back door when she let the dog outside.

The sliding doors opened and Freckles darted out, raced around him, barking and wagging her tail.

Jen started to the close the door, but Logan got the toe of his boot inside, grabbed the handle, and pulled it open. Her little antic would be amusing if she didn't look so stricken. Eye makeup ran in black streaks down her face. Seeing her so miserable wrenched his heart.

The dog jumped on him one more time, before giving up and bounding off further into the back yard. Logan pulled the glass door shut behind him. This would go better without the distractions Freckles created, or so he hoped.

He'd prepared a speech, but now he couldn't remember the words.

"You don't have to wag your tail, but you could act a little happier to see me."

She wiped her face with a tissue. He thought he saw a smile begin to form, but it didn't quite make it to her eyes. "I'm sorry about trying to close the door on you. That was juvenile."

"Why did you leave so fast? Did Huston say something that upset you?"

Her forehead creased in a perplexed frown. "Who?"

"The guy who took you to your seat. He's my brother, Huston. I thought he introduced himself."

"No, he didn't. He did ask if I had any ugly stepsisters. Maybe he didn't think it was important for me to know him, considering..."

"Considering what?"

"That we won't be seeing each other again."

"You don't have to see my wise-ass brother again if you don't want to."

"I'm not talking about your brother."

"Yeah, I know. But I'm not leaving town without apologizing for the things I said to you. I was angry, but that's no excuse for hurting you."

"You didn't say anything I don't deserve." Jen's coolness didn't fool him. She put up that defense when she was afraid. He didn't want her to be scared anymore. He wanted to soothe her fears, and deal with whatever had sent her running again. Giving in to the urge to put his arms around her, he took a step in her direction.

She backed away. "Please, Logan. Don't make this any harder than it has to be."

He held out his arms. "This doesn't have to be hard, Jen, if you would just give it a chance."

Fear flashed across her face. "You and I have an agreement. You gave me your word."

Logan dropped his hands to his sides with a frustrated

huff. That damn deal had become her weapon. "I know what I promised, but, damn it, Jan, I can't just walk away and never see you again…and you aren't being honest if you say you want me to."

She went to the sliding glass doors, giving him a better view of her backside. That black dress showed off her assets, and there were many. He considered pulling up the hem, exposing her thighs, and running his hands over her incredibly smooth skin. He'd take her to bed and love on her until she screamed his name, and admitted she wanted him as badly as he wanted her.

Holding back took all his willpower. He wouldn't use physical attraction to manipulate her; it wouldn't work even if he did. He had to find out why she wouldn't let herself consider a future with him. In his heart, he knew she had feelings for him.

"Am I right?"

"Yes," she said softly. "I don't want to say goodbye. But I know it's the best thing for both of us if we do." She hugged herself. God, he wished she would let him hold her. He wished she would let him in.

"I don't get it. What we did, what we have, it's more than just good sex and we both know it. So tell me how you figure throwing this away is the best thing?"

"What you said about friendship and love, I can't trust like that. I've tried, but I can't." She spoke with so much conviction he almost believed her. *She* believed what she said. Something in her past had wounded her so deeply that she'd closed her heart. If he could find out what, maybe he could help her get past it.

"Who hurt you?"

"You'll think it's ridiculous."

"Anything that hurt you so bad you can't trust me, is far from ridiculous."

For a long while she was silent, and when she did begin to speak, her voice was so low that he had to move closer to hear. "I was very shy growing up. It was hard for me to make friends, and we moved a lot, so I didn't have many. When I got into high school, I met a guy named Ryan. He was outgoing and good-looking and popular. All the things I wasn't…"

She couldn't still think so little of herself. "You're a beautiful woman, Jen."

"Thank you." She cast a grateful look over her shoulder, but he didn't want her gratitude. He wanted her to believe in herself, and to believe in him. "I was a stick in high school. My boobs were smaller than a guy's."

"Define stick. The kids on the basketball team called me Praying Mantis because of my long, skinny arms. I grew so fast in high school, I looked like a freak."

Her gaze flickered over him. The craving in her eyes heated his blood. "That's not a word that comes to mind when I look at you."

"Stick isn't how I'd describe you either. Remind me later to show you in detail how beautiful you are." High school awkwardness might explain a few insecurities, but it wouldn't account for her intense fears. Something else had happened. "You were telling me about Ryan."

"Ryan, right…" She brushed at her hair with her fingers, though not a strand was out of place. He'd noticed she did that when she got anxious. "He asked me for help with homework. Somehow, from there, we became friends. I'd never had a boyfriend, or even a good friend who was a guy, and it was really flattering that this popular, good-looking one wanted to hang out with me. After a while, he asked if I'd go out with him, you know, be his girlfriend. I said yes, but then I got freaked out and broke it off after a couple days.

"He wouldn't talk to me for a week. I was miserable, and all the girls were telling me what a huge mistake I'd made. So I went over to his house to see if we could still be friends. He apologized for ignoring me, and said it was because he liked me so much and I'd hurt him. He kissed me. I didn't push him away, even though in hindsight I should have. I thought maybe I was wrong to break up. Maybe I'd like him like that, if I gave it a try. I-I let him touch me, but when he started taking off my clothes, I got scared. When I tried to push him away, he accused me of being a tease and he…he…"

Jen faced the sliding glass door, finishing in silence what she wasn't able to say.

Logan's blood boiled. "Did he rape you? Tell me, Jen. It won't change what I think about you, or how I feel. You need to tell me the truth because you need to get that weight off your shoulders. Let me help you carry it."

Her hands curled around her upper arms, a protective self-hug. "His parents came home and they caught us before he could…you know, penetrate me. I was so embarrassed and crying so hard I couldn't talk. He told them I wanted it, that I'd been trying to get him into bed."

Her tone had gone flat, but it didn't lessen the impact, which was like a sledgehammer to Logan's chest. "That son-of-a-bitch. I hope you got him arrested."

"They called my mother to come get me. She didn't get mad or threaten to go to the police when I told her what happened. Her face went stiff, like a mask. She said we had to keep it quiet, that making a fuss would only make things worse because it would be his word against mine. She told me, 'Men are like that. You shouldn't lead them on.' "

Logan clenched his fists, fighting the urge to take Jen into his arms and vow to protect her. He couldn't protect her from what had happened in the past, and if he touched her, she would freeze up and refuse to talk. "Your mother was wrong. All men *aren't* like that, but *none* of what happened was your fault. You have to know that."

Her shoulders lifted as she breathed deeply, then exhaled. "Ryan turned on me. He told his friends I'd hit on him and got him in trouble. The other guys whispered awful things to me in the hallway, like asking me to give them blowjobs. Some of them tried to put their hands on me when teachers weren't around. The girls acted different too.

They gossiped behind my back, even when they knew I could hear them. Denying the lies didn't change anything. Ryan's friends stood up for him. I was new at the school, and I didn't have many friends. After that, I didn't want anyone to get close. I was afraid they might betray me too."

"Where the hell was your dad during all this? If that happened to a daughter of mine, I'd take a shotgun to the bastard."

"I don't know what my mother told him, because I was too ashamed to talk about it. They eventually moved me to an all-girls boarding school, and never brought it up again." She turned slightly and looked at him over her shoulder. "You were right when you suggested I need help."

He wanted to kick himself. "No, I was an asshole. I shouldn't have said that—"

"But you're *right*. I'm messed up, Logan. Something's broken inside, and I can't fix it. I've seen doctors and I've taken medicine and tried special treatments. I still fight anxiety, and I'm afraid to let anyone get close. Over the past ten years, I've dated two men, one of them somewhat seriously, but he broke up with me because I wouldn't sleep with him, and I wouldn't commit. It's not just what happened with Ryan; it's how I grew up. I never knew..." Her voice cracked. "I don't think my parents knew how to love me. You're the first man I've let this close, and I know I'm being stupid by pushing you away, but I can't seem to help it."

Tears slid down her cheeks and he felt every one of them, like she was dripping acid onto his heart.

He gave up trying to keep his hands to himself and drew her against him. "You're not stupid. You're beautiful and brilliant, and sweet and tenderhearted, and passionate as hell, and that's only what I've discovered in one week. Just think about what I'll find when we spend more time together."

She circled her arms around his waist. "That's what

scares me. You'll find out too much, and you'll leave. Everyone leaves eventually."

Her prediction tore away another piece of his heart.

If ever a woman needed loving, Jen did, and the way she was clinging to him just proved how much she needed his love. But if he pursued this, he would have to risk everything. His future. His heart. And he'd have to trust her even before she trusted him.

"I know how scary it is to care for someone. I haven't been willing to let myself care too much either, because I didn't want to risk getting hurt. Not after losing two people I loved so much." He rubbed his hand in a soothing circle on her back. "You know what I said about my folks being best friends? There's another side to that. I saw what my mother's death did to my father. He stopped living. He gets up every morning and he works until dark, but he doesn't enjoy life. He's hard and bitter. I don't want to end up like that. I thought I could give just a little, not everything, and that way I could avoid what happened to him.

"But I've been thinking these past couple days, and I realize that's not how I want it to be. I want what my parents had. I want it all, even if it means risking everything. And if you...if you want it all too, we could make this work." Logan kissed the top of her head. If he kept talking, he was pretty sure he would get choked up.

He'd said his piece, and she'd heard him. He hoped she would take courage from his words and fight her fears. If she wouldn't, or couldn't, there was nothing more he could do.

Chapter Ten

Logan had to be one of the few true gentlemen left in the world. Possibly others like him existed. Maybe they lived in Texas. Jen hadn't spent much time there. However, she'd met enough men to know this one was special. By some miracle, he cared about her, and he wanted to deepen the relationship.

Jen splayed her fingers over his back, loving his solidness and how secure she felt when she was with him. She adored his slow drawl and even slower lovemaking, as well as his quick wit, and easy-going personality. She wanted nothing more than to say yes, and take the leap. Only, there were obstacles beyond her irrational fears. She longed to listen to her heart, but she'd better heed her common sense.

"What are your plans for the future, Logan? I thought you wanted to go back to school and become a vet?"

"I do. But we can work around that." He slid his fingers through her hair, stroking. If she remained in his arms for much longer, she wouldn't be able resist taking him to bed again. After that, the bonds between them would be tighter, stronger. She feared they might already be too strong to cut without permanent injury.

"What if we can't work around it? I'm settled in Atlanta. You said you plan to finish your schooling at Texas A&M. I don't see how this can work if we're in different states." She hated how logical and cold she sounded. He'd opened his heart to her, and had asked her to do the same. She would have to go into this relationship without guarantees, only his assurance. "If there's a baby, and things don't work out, our child would be the one who suffers most. I can't take the chance."

He tightened his embrace. "I won't abandon you and the baby. That's a promise."

"You can't make a promise like that when you don't know for certain what will happen."

"We'll figure it out. Together."

She knew he meant it. But believing in his sincerity and being able to stake her life on it were two different things. She extracted herself from his arms.

He didn't look pleased. "You don't believe me?"

No, she was terrified he might actually convince her. "I believe you're sincere, but you aren't looking at this logically."

"I'm not accepting your excuses. There's a difference."

"You aren't being practical." She hated being practical, except she didn't see that she had much choice. "This isn't some chick flick or romance novel, where everything magically works out in spite of insurmountable differences."

He closed his eyes and rubbed his forehead. "I'm not suggesting believing in fairy tales. I know it won't be easy."

Tears burned behind her eyes. If she started crying, he'd hold her again, and she didn't have the strength to push him away. She blinked until the moisture cleared and forced neutrality into her voice. "Am I giving you a headache?"

Logan dropped his arm, his expression turning solemn. Normally, he'd be the one cracking a joke right about now. Fatigue had etched lines on his face, and his eyes reflected sadness, and more than that, pain. "Don't do this, Jen. Don't talk yourself out of it."

She whirled away before giving in to the overwhelming desire to throw her arms around him. He was hurting, and she was the cause. That's why this couldn't last. She refused to continue to wound him because she was too scared to love him. It would tear both of them apart.

Crossing to the kitchen desk, she took an envelope from one of the cubbyholes, then returned to him and held it out. At least she could help him fulfill his dream. "Here's what I promised you. Go back to Texas and become a vet. If, after that, you still want to work things out, we'll give it a try."

He flicked a look at the envelope. Disbelief flashed in his eyes, but then his gaze went flat. "Keep it…or put it in a college fund for junior." Logan then spun on his heel and left.

The sliding door remained open, but he wouldn't be back. She would bet on it.

Jen bit her knuckle. She had to do something to distract herself from the excruciating pain in her chest. *Oh God, it hurt.* She'd done the right thing by sending him away. Before he could hurt her, and before she hurt him even more than she already had.

Liar. She hadn't done it because it was right, or even logical. She'd pushed him away because she was a coward. The idea of loving him scared her to death.

Wasn't she already close to loving him? Avoiding it was like trying to avoid raindrops when it rained. The skies had opened. Logan had pried her fingers from around the handle of her umbrella, taking away her false security, offering to be her shelter. She'd thrown away her opportunity for true happiness because she was afraid of getting wet.

Jen rushed out the back door to catch him before he made it to the neighbor's yard. Letting him go wasn't right or smart, it would be the stupidest mistake she'd ever made. She had to stop him, tell him he'd been right about her all along, and beg him for another chance.

She ran off the patio and threw the gate open. "Logan! Wait!"

A flash of black and white flashed in her peripheral vision. Her dog bounded into the front yard, tail waving, looking around expectantly. At the sidewalk, Freckles jerked to an abrupt halt, her attention focused on something across the street. A squirrel. *Of course, what else?* The oblivious little creature furiously dug at the dirt beneath a thick-limbed oak tree.

From the neighboring driveway, a car engine roared to life, and a gleaming gray sedan backed into the street, one of the wedding guests leaving early. Jen's lungs seized. Freckles had no fear of cars, and wouldn't notice it anyway, her attention being fastened on the squirrel.

Jen wobbled as she ran. *Damn heels.* She kicked off her shoes. "Freckles, sit!"

The dog might obey that command. She got treats when she sat.

Not today.

Freckles took off as if shot from a cannon, racing across the street, chasing the squirrel around the base of the tree. The dog braced her paws on the trunk when her prey dashed into the branches, and her white-tipped tail went into a wagging frenzy. What was it about squirrel behavior that made her think they wanted to play?

"Stay!"

The last command penetrated the dog's one-track mind, but instead of staying put, the foolish mutt pranced back toward the road, panting with satisfaction. The driver wouldn't see her dart out from between the cars, which were parked up and down both sides of the street.

Until this point, Jen hadn't panicked. Now, all bets were off.

"No! Stay! *Stay!*"

A tall figure dashed past her. Logan, in his formal suit, sprinted into the road, waving his arms at the car, yelling at the driver. *What the hell was he doing?*

"You idiot! Stop!" Jen screamed at the driver, at Logan, and at the dog.

Tires screeched. A sickening thud, followed by Logan tumbling over the hood, stopped her heart.

She stared in horror at the car, no longer able to see Logan. *Was he on the other side? Oh, God, under the tires?* With a loud cry, she broke into a dead run. "No, no, no! Please God, no…"

The car door swung open and out leapt a well-dressed man with a shocked expression. "What the…?" Loud music throbbed from the car's interior. No wonder the driver hadn't heard Logan shouting.

She raced around the front end.

Logan sat back on his heels, appearing dazed, but not seriously injured.

Relief hit so hard it buckled her knees. She knelt next to him, longing to drag him into her arms, to hold him and never let him go. If he was injured, jostling him might cause more damage. She put a trembling hand on his shoulder. "Logan—" Her voice broke.

"Hey man, are you all right? I didn't see you until you were in front of me." The driver's shaken voice came from over her shoulder. He held a phone in his hand.

So that's what the idiot had been doing instead of paying attention. Jen longed to grab that phone and shove it up his ass. "If you'd been watching what you were doing, you would've seen him. Call 9-1-1."

"I'm okay," Logan rasped. "Get the dog."

The dog. That was why he'd run into the street. In that instant, everything had been wiped from her mind, except for Logan. He could've been killed trying to save her dog. *Oh, Logan.* How could any man be so softhearted? Without him, the world would be harder and crueler than she'd ever imagined.

Freckles crouched on the sidewalk with her head between her paws, her dark eyes imploring, as if she'd figured out, finally, that she had caused a shit-storm.

"Come here." Jen kept her voice low and calm. If she yelled, the dog would get scared and run.

Freckles crept over and sniffed Logan's bleeding palms. Jen grabbed hold of the dog's collar and pulled her away so she wouldn't try to lick him. "You're not okay, you're hurt."

"I'm fine," Logan insisted. "It's only a few scrapes."

"But he hit you."

"No, I tried to jump out of the way and hit the hood. Rolled off. He wasn't going that fast." Logan slowly got to his feet. "See? Nothing broken."

Jen lifted the twenty-pound dog and held Freckles against her shoulder with one arm. The little sycophant bathed her face. Using her other hand, she steadied Logan and continued to hold onto him, even after it was clear he didn't need her help. His tan tuxedo was torn in several places and dirty at the knees where he'd knelt on the pavement. Other than the scrapes on his hands, he appeared unhurt, which was a miracle.

Her stomach still churned as her mind replayed the moment Logan tumbled over the car's hood. She studied his face, the flushed skin, and the distant look in his eyes. "If you won't go to the hospital, you need to get those cuts tended. Come back to the house. I've got hydrogen peroxide and bandages."

"Is there anything I can do?" the driver asked in a worried tone. He probably feared being sued.

"Pay better attention." Jen flung the suggestion over her shoulder, still hugging Logan's arm as they walked together back to her house. The accident wasn't wholly the driver's fault, but she couldn't help getting angry, and needed to direct it somewhere besides at Logan. *What had he been thinking to run in front of that car?* He must've presumed the driver would see him and stop. He'd put his faith in someone undeserving.

Right. He'd put his faith in her too, and look where that had gotten him.

Her insides remained knotted, and the tightness in her throat wouldn't go away, no matter how many times she swallowed. She wouldn't blame him if he didn't want anything more to do with her.

Once she was inside the gate, she put Freckles down. "Go find a squirrel in your own yard."

The music coming from the other side of the hedges had shifted from Mozart to metal. The party was just getting underway. Logan hesitated and glanced in the direction of the festivities. "I need to get back."

Once again, he wasn't considering his own needs. He didn't want to offend his friend by not returning. The fact he'd left the reception to come talk to her spoke volumes about how he felt. Or *had* felt. Could be past tense.

She eyed him worriedly. His face was less flushed, actually, now he looked pale. He could be hurt worse than he thought. "I wish you'd let me take you to a doctor."

He frowned. "Jen, I'll be all right. I'm just a little shook up."

"Really? Well, I'm a *lot* 'shook up.' Look, I know you need to go, but I'd feel better if you would at least come inside and let me put some salve on those cuts."

"Fine, all right." Logan allowed her to take his arm and lead him into the house, even though his frown remained. *Who wouldn't be grumpy after being run over?* He hadn't snapped at the driver though. His mood might have more to do with her and the way they'd parted. He'd offered her his heart — and she'd given him a check. If he'd been any other man except Logan, he would've pushed *her* in front of the car.

She indicated a stool at the breakfast bar. "Sit there while I get the first aid kit."

He sat as requested, but before she made it past him, he stopped her. "Why did you come after me?"

Her watch buzzed. *Stupid thing, had the worst timing...* If she ended her conversation with Logan now to take a conference call, she wouldn't get a second chance. Or was it a third? He'd given her so many chances she didn't deserve. In only a few days, Logan had shown her how different her life could be, how wonderful, if she would drop her guard and be willing to open her heart.

She removed the watch and dropped it into a drawer, slamming it shut. "You were right. I've been making excuses to avoid being hurt. I haven't known many people in my life that I could depend on, not even my parents, so it's hard for me to trust. I'm not good at it. But I'm willing to try, because...because I think you're worth it."

Logan's expression softened, but he still didn't say anything. Maybe he knew she wasn't finished with what she had to tell him, or he wasn't willing to risk more than he already had.

She clasped her hands in front of her, needing something to hold onto, and not quite sure he was willing to let her hold onto him. "I should've told you before how much I admire you. You're a man of rare insight and sensitivity. A lot smarter than I thought you were when I first met you, and more patient than I deserve...and you're a sap when it comes to dogs." Nervous, she looked down at her hands. "I guess what I'm trying to say is..."

Get a backbone, Jen. Look at him when you tell him. With Logan sitting on the stool and her standing, they were closer to the same height. She met his direct gaze. The answer would be there, in his eyes. His beautiful blue eyes. "I think I could love you, cowboy. I know I can't bear the thought of losing you. What do you say we give this a chance?"

Chapter Eleven

Double H Ranch, North Central Texas

Six weeks after Logan returned to Texas, Jen got on a plane and flew out to see him. She'd talked to him every night since he'd left Atlanta, and had counted the minutes until she could see him again. She ran to meet him in the airport. He picked her up, whirling her around, before giving her a very private kiss in public. Then he drove to a hotel downtown, where they checked in and promptly went to bed — in the middle of the afternoon. They stayed there until the next morning, when he suggested they go out for breakfast.

As he sat on the edge of the bed, deliciously naked, she wrapped her arms around him and rubbed her cheek on his shoulder. Her hand drifted downward. "Are you sure you don't want room service?"

He pulled her into his lap, nuzzling her neck while he played with her breasts. "What I'm hungry for, they don't serve."

She threaded her fingers through his dark-blonde hair, and whispered in his ear. "Give me your order, and I'll see what I can do."

After another round of lovemaking, they showered together and got dressed in between kisses. She pulled on a sleeveless black shirt and ran her hands over the front of her skinny jeans. Her body gave no indication she carried a child, but it was still very early.

The home pregnancy test had come back positive. Next week, she had a doctor's appointment and could confirm the positive result, although she'd already calculated a due date. She'd debated telling Logan, but decided it would be better to wait until she was certain everything was all right — the baby *and* their relationship.

A future together was by no means a given, although she was committed to trying. Thankfully, Logan hadn't dropped off the face of the earth, as she feared he might. That didn't mean something couldn't happen to spoil everything. Most likely it would be her fault, because he was too sweet and honorable to screw it all up.

She eyed his backside as he buttoned his jeans. "Have I ever told you that you have a hot ass?"

"Mm, a few times." He drew her to him for a kiss and ran his hands over her behind. "Yours gets my vote, along with all the other parts."

"We could do an inventory of our favorite parts." She hoped he'd take her suggestion and they could crawl back into bed.

He hesitated before putting on his t-shirt with an apologetic smile. "I told Austin we'd be downstairs by nine. He said he'd have breakfast with us before we head out to the ranch. Everybody's eager to meet you."

"Too bad. Maybe later. I'm sure you're hungry." She cupped his bristly cheeks, giving him a deep kiss and ending it with a tender smooch. This relationship was still so new that she didn't want anyone else to be a part of it yet. And what if his family didn't like her? What then?

He brushed her hair back and gazed into her eyes. "Something wrong?"

"I'm nervous about meeting your family." She might as

well admit it. Logan would figure it out anyway. He had an uncanny ability to pick up on her emotions, and sometimes even her thoughts. She'd told him about her anxiety, which she'd tried to conquer with therapy, meds, and even diet and exercise. Some of it had helped, but she had a long way to go. Would Logan tire of dealing with her fears? She was anxious about that too.

He gave her an encouraging smile. "Don't worry about meeting my family. They'll love you."

Logan had given her the same answer before when she'd expressed concern, and he'd told her to be herself. If she did that, his family would ask her leave. She was self-aware enough to know she wasn't an easy person to like. Her co-workers had called her the Iron Maiden behind her back, until Angela threatened them with bodily harm. How had she attracted a man as perfect as Logan? She had to pinch herself every so often, so she'd know she wasn't dreaming.

Downstairs, they were shown to a table by a window, where a man waited for them who bore a strong resemblance to Logan, except for his dark hair. He'd pushed his chair back and sat casually with his ankle resting on his knee, revealing faded jeans and black cowboy boots. The sleeves of his blue-and-white checkered shirt were rolled up to his elbows. He looked more like a country boy than a city chef.

He stood as they approached, and a grin broke out right before Logan hauled him into a bear hug. "Cookie, how's it goin'?"

"All good." His brother returned the hug, before he turned to her, almost as if he expected *her* to give him a hug too. She wasn't brave enough to initiate it, so she shook his hand. "Hi…Jen Chandler."

"I'm Austin. The *handsome* brother." Where Logan's eyes were sky blue, his younger brother's eye color reminded her of the deep ocean. Here was another heartbreaker, and the smart aleck gene had to run in the family.

"The string of broken hearts must be long indeed." she replied.

"All he has to do is cook for them. Makes it way too easy," Logan muttered, as if annoyed. He knew full well, all he had to do was put on those ass-hugging jeans to attract a crowd of drooling women.

"Thank you," Jen murmured. After she was seated, Logan and Austin took their respective seats, and it appeared they were waiting for her to say something. Still nervous, she opted for the obvious conversation starter, however lame. "Logan tells me you're sous chef at the four-star restaurant here in the hotel."

Austin tipped his chin in acknowledgment. "On the top floor. If you come back for dinner, I'll bake you a *soufflé*."

"You never offered to bake *me* a soufflé," Logan complained.

"You aren't as pretty as she is." Austin lifted a black carafe and looked her way, raising his eyebrows. "Coffee?"

"Yes, thank you."

This wasn't so bad. Logan was being Logan, and his brother was just as quick with the banter, as well as being attentive, but not overly, so she didn't feel scrutinized.

Austin poured steaming coffee into the white china cup in front of her. "Has my brother made you a proper meal yet?"

Logan laughed through his nose. "Jen's cooking is better than mine."

"Then we're in trouble," she murmured under her breath.

"She's humble, too…and sweet." Smiling, he filled up his cup, adding cream, no sugar. He'd admitted to liking strong coffee and sweet girls, and it made her wonder again what had attracted him to her. She was far from sweet, and he knew it.

"You could take a couple days off and come out to the ranch," he said to Austin. "Miss Kate would let you take over the kitchen."

"No thanks." Austin's flat tone left no room for

negotiation, and neither did the expression on his face. She assumed his attitude stemmed from the reaction he'd gotten from his other brothers regarding his career choice. How telling that Logan chose to introduce her to Austin before they went to meet the rest of the family.

A pony-tailed waitress stopped by and asked for their order. Austin waited until she and Logan had given theirs, before he spoke. "Thanks, I'll pass. I have to leave soon."

Maybe she shouldn't have ordered that big omelet if they were in a hurry.

"What's up?" Logan appeared surprised. "I thought you said we'd have breakfast together."

"Sorry, Loco, I hate stepping out on you and your lady friend." Austin gave Jen a regretful smile. "We have a new manager and she wants to meet the restaurant staff pronto. Just got her call. Would've been nice to have more notice."

"Isn't this your day off? That's not very considerate."

Jen looked away from Logan's disapproving frown, sipping her coffee in silence. She'd made similar demands of her team, although she never asked others to do what she wasn't willing to do herself. Still, Logan had somehow gotten the impression she had tender heart. Her co-workers would find that hilarious.

Austin slid his chair away from the table. "Miss Claire Banks, the new boss, is from England. Maybe that's the way they do things across the pond." He tipped his head in Jen's direction. "Nice to meet you, Jen. I'm looking forward to getting to know you better. Any friend of Loco's is a friend of mine. You be sure to convince him to bring you back early, I promise, you won't regret it."

"I know I won't. It was nice to meet you, too."

After Austin's departure, she turned to Logan. "Loco?"

He shrugged. "We all have nicknames. I was the least crazy, thus, I got the name Loco."

"Of course. Makes perfect sense."

After breakfast, they started on what Logan said would

be a two-hour drive to the ranch. She watched out the window of his pickup truck as they traveled from cityscape to countryside, past green pastures to rugged range. They talked, listened to music, played silly games to pass the time, and then talked some more. Logan was the only person she could imagine accompanying on a cross-country road trip and not getting bored.

He eventually left the highway for a two-lane road, and began to execute a series of right and left turns, until they were out in the middle of nowhere. They passed a herd of cattle with distinctive curving horns. She straightened. "I've never seen Texas longhorns up close. They look enormous."

"Aw, that's just an illusion. Longhorns are actually puny and shy. Texas Aggies are bigger and braver. They'll come right up and introduce themselves."

She was about to ask him how to recognize the *Aggies* breed until it struck her he was talking about college mascots. "Yes, I've noticed *Aggies* can be overly friendly."

"If I didn't know better, I'd think you went to U-T."

"I attended Yale."

He gave her an apologetic smile. "My condolences on not being able to get into A&M."

"You're only sorry because you didn't meet me sooner."

"True enough, though I'm pretty sure you wouldn't have given me the time of day if your mind wasn't on genetics."

There, he had it wrong. She would've been just as awe-struck. Her first impression of him had thrown her for a loop, or as he might say, *knocked her off her horse*. From the moment he'd made friends with her dog, she hadn't been able to stop thinking about him.

Jen gazed out the window, a little alarmed by how fast she'd fallen, and how hard. "I couldn't possibly ignore you after your kind offer to trim my bush."

His low chuckle drew her attention. "That's got to be the worst first impressions I ever made. I'm surprised you didn't grab the pruning shears and chase me out of your yard."

"The thought did enter my mind. I decided to ask you out instead."

"You're a smart woman."

"Humility is one of the things about you that most attracts me," she replied smoothly.

"Don't forget my *hot ass*."

"How could I?" She put her hand over her smile, recalling how he'd looked this morning coming out of the shower—in a word, *yummy*. Maybe after meeting the family, they could slip away to bed early. "When will we get to the ranch?"

He turned off the pavement and gravel crunched beneath the tires. "We've been driving around it for the past half hour."

"Seriously?" She looked outside again. "How big is it?"

"A paltry hundred thousand acres."

Her jaw dropped. "Paltry?"

"The largest ranches in Texas are more than three times that size."

"That's hard to imagine." She shook her head in disbelief. "Where are the fences?"

"We put up fences along the main roads. Out here, we don't need them. Texas is an open range state. Cattle can go where they need to graze. We round them up if they wander too far."

Jen surveyed the rugged landscape, blanketed by wild grasses and trees, the distinctive mesquite being the most recognizable. "This is like stepping into a time machine."

"Things haven't changed all that much out here…as far as the land goes." Logan implied things had changed in other ways, but he didn't elaborate.

He slowed the truck as they reached a stone gateway with a wrought iron arch that encompassed the family brand Logan had described: interlocking hearts around a double H. When he turned the wheels and drove through the open gate, the tires sent a cloud of dust into the air, partially obscuring the arch reflected in the rear side mirror. It was funny, how seeing the actual emblem and remembering the story behind it made her pulse race. Was that how the first woman who'd seen it had felt when her husband presented her with a powerful symbol of his love?

"I remember what you told me about the origin of the double hearts brand. Do all the men in your family have your ancestor's romantic streak?"

Logan threw back his head and belly laughed.

"I take that as a *no*."

"We're about as romantic as those longhorns you just saw."

"Really? You could've fooled me."

Logan was one of the most romantic men she'd ever met. Not in the gushy, traditional sense. His romantic overtures were authentic and earthy, and laced with humor. She suspected Austin possessed similar traits, and wondered whether his brothers were like that, as well. If they were, meeting them might not be so intimidating.

The truck crested a hill, and she caught her breath at the picturesque panorama: rolling grassland, as far as she could see. There were fences here, which were made of metal pipe, not barbed wire, and horses grazed, rather than the cows she'd seen earlier.

They must be getting close to his home. She tried to ignore the pressure building in her chest, which signaled anxiety, and focused her mind on the healthy excitement, and on her curiosity about the ranch.

Out in the middle of a pasture someone had erected a curious collection of buildings, what looked like shipping containers with false fronts attached. Jen could make out a sign, General Store, and next door, a saloon, and one of the little buildings looked like a church, complete with steeple. The path that led out there had been fenced off and the gate, locked. "What's over there?" she pointed. "It looks like a movie set."

Logan barely glanced in the direction she indicated. "It's a replica of an old western town...my mother's idea. She wanted to attract folks out here to celebrate things like weddings and family reunions. Convinced my father to build that little town so she'd have somewhere to stage the events."

"Did it work?"

Sadness ghosted Logan's features. "She died shortly after it got built. Dad hasn't done anything with it since. We have a few regulars who come out here to hunt, but that's all."

How sad that his mother didn't live to see her idea reach fruition.

"What are the buildings used for now?"

"Nothing, just storage."

"Do you think your family will do anything with them?"

"Hard to say. Dad stays busy operating the ranch. He's not opposed to bringing in more money, but my mom wanted to turn the Double H into some kind of rustic resort, combined with the working ranch, and make it...I don't know...*romantic*." Logan's smile quickly faded. "She was the romantic one. None of us guys have the least idea about how to make something like that work."

Jen could see the potential in his mother's idea, and it was something she could help with...that is, if Logan would accept her help. "There's no reason it couldn't work. You aren't that far away from a major metropolitan area and a large airport. For that matter, you have enough land for an airstrip, if guests wanted to rent a charter plane. If you build it *and market it*, people will come."

"Yeah, maybe." He shook his head. " Without mom to lead it, I don't see how it'll happen."

As they passed what remained of his mother's vision, Jen's mind continued to whir. She didn't know jack about ranching, but she knew marketing, and if she could come up with helpful suggestions for how to turn the forlorn little town into a romance retreat, that should make a good impression on his family. Even if Logan wasn't interested in running it—after all, he had his own dreams—someone else might be.

Just beyond the little town, they took another hill, and more buildings came into view: a barn, stables, corrals, and other structures she couldn't name, but that looked typical to ranches. After they'd passed a large pond, Logan took a fork in the road and headed up a hill in the direction of a two-story farmhouse. The other road ended at a mid-century modern ranch-style home.

"Who lives out here?"

"My dad lives in the ranch house, that's where us boys grew up. Huston's living there now, too, and Clay sleeps there when he's not doing the rodeo circuit. Jake just moved back in. Dad grew up in the big house, my grandparent's house, which dates back to the turn of the century. It was built on the site of the original homestead. A few years ago, we renovated the bedrooms and added bathrooms so we could take in guests. But like I said, we aren't really advertising. That's where you'll stay."

Surprised, Jen jerked her head around to look at him. "Where *I'll* stay? What about you?"

"I'll sleep at the other house. My grandmother is old-fashioned."

Jen frowned. Two women in that huge house, with all those men in the smaller one, made no sense at all, and she had expected to be with Logan each precious moment of the long weekend. If they weren't living nearly a thousand miles away from each other, it wouldn't be such a big deal. But if she suggested they room together, his grandmother would consider her a slut. Her hopes for spending hours in Logan's arms sank like a day-old helium-filled balloon.

"So, we won't be together." She couldn't hide her disappointment.

"We won't sleep in the same room. That doesn't mean

we can't be together in other *interesting* places." He arched his eyebrows suggestively.

"Where?" she scoffed. "In a hay stack?"

"Hay stacks are underappreciated."

She scrunched her nose. "Oh no…"

"We'll find places to hide out. You'll just have to trust me."

Logan clearly had no idea how *much* she trusted him. She hated going to the dentist more than anything, but she would rather get her teeth drilled than be presented to his family like a prize cow. Even so, she'd agreed to come out here because she wanted to please him.

Nausea swept over her in a wave. *Panic?* No, she wasn't freaking out, no way. Meeting Austin, however briefly, hadn't been a bad experience. Plus, she had a good idea for how to make a positive impression. Everything would work out.

He pulled up in a gravel lot next to the two-story house, where several other vehicles were parked. "That's dad's truck, and Huston's is next to his, and there's my grandmother's pink Cadillac. Pops bought it for her at an auction years ago, and she won't drive anything else. The old green pickup belongs to Clay, and Jake has the patrol car. I texted them about what time we'd arrive."

The front door opened, and a petite white-haired woman came out onto the porch, looking trim in dark slacks and a simple white button-up shirt. Following her were three men, who towered over her, two of them dark-haired and one sandy-haired, all dressed like cowboys.

Logan smiled and waved. "See? I told you. They're eager to meet you."

Nausea struck again, and Jen's mouth watered. Not from panic, this was different. She hadn't experienced a whiff of morning sickness before now, but…she had better find a bathroom, quick. Her stomach lurched, and her breakfast came up the same way it had gone down, only tasting way worse. Oh no, she couldn't wait. She threw open the passenger door, leaned out, and vomited onto the gravel.

Logan kept his arm around Jen's shoulders as he guided her inside the house and into the front room. She'd admitted earlier to being nervous, but he hadn't realized she was so anxious she would get sick.

"Here, sit down," He plopped next to her on a leather couch, one of two in the large room that served as a congregating area for the family and anyone else who stayed there. Right now, Jen was the only guest.

In her usual no-nonsense manner, Miss Kate snatched up a bowl of peppermint candy set out on a side table. She dropped a disc into Jen's outstretched hand. "Have a peppermint, honey. It'll settle your stomach."

"Thank you. That should help." Jen popped the candy into her mouth.

Logan hugged her with one arm, not knowing what else to do. He typically kept his head when someone was hurt or ailing, but seeing Jen turn pale and get sick had made his insides twist and his brain turn to mush. "Is there anything I can get you?"

"I'm fine, really," she whispered.

She didn't look fine. He took her hand—*clammy*. Nope, she wasn't fine. "Rest here a minute until you're sure."

Huston perched on the edge of a nearby chair. Clay and Jake stationed themselves by the mantle, looking like they'd rather be anywhere else. Jake had on his deputy's uniform, so he must've left work on a lunch break. He met Logan's gaze and his coal-black eyebrows formed a questioning arch. Was he curious about what had brought on Jen's sudden illness? More likely he wondered when the food would be served. Clay rested his elbow on the stone mantle and propped one booted foot on the hearth. He hadn't removed his hat and had his head down. Trying not to laugh? The awkward scene would've been funny, only there was nothing amusing about poor Jen's greenish skin tone.

Maybe she had food poisoning. Logan silently vowed he'd kill Austin if she ended up at the hospital after eating at the hotel, whether he had anything to do with it or not.

Their father had escaped to the kitchen, saying he'd fetch a glass of water. After he returned and handed her the glass, he joined Jake and Clay by the fireplace, as far away from her as possible, while still remaining in the same room. She wasn't carrying the plague, for God's sake.

"Would you feel better if you could lie down?" His grandmother's tone remained solicitous, but Jen winced.

"I'm so sorry," she murmured.

"No need to be sorry." Logan kept his arm around her shoulders, protecting her.

Huston leaned forward and rested his arms on his knees. "Now if you'd puked in my new boots, like Logan did one time, you'd have something to be sorry about. He never did apologize."

A smile played around Jen's mouth.

Logan heaved a relieved sigh. *Thank goodness for Huston and his warped sense of humor.*

"I remember that trip," Logan mused. "Dad was driving up into the mountains…"

Jake gave a dry laugh. "Be glad you didn't puke in *my* boots."

"Wouldn't have made any difference if he'd puked in your boots. They always stunk to high heaven," Clay said under his breath, but loud enough to be heard.

Logan decided he needed to clarify a point. "I was ten at the time,"

"Still, you owe me an apology," Huston insisted. "And a new pair of boots."

"Put it on my bill."

Huston rested his arms on the chair and leaned back, like his job was done. He'd taken the attention off Jen's predicament and everyone seemed a lot more relaxed, including Jen.

While she sipped at her water, Logan introduced his family. "You've met Huston. No need to introduce him again."

Huston made an offended expression. "Hey, you didn't tell her I'm your *favorite* brother."

"You're a pain in my—"

Miss Kate cleared her throat.

He wouldn't have cussed, not too much anyway. "Jen, this is my grandmother, Katherine Parker Hardt."

"Call me Miss Kate. Everybody else does. It's good to finally meet you, dear."

Jen returned the smile. "I'm glad to meet you, too. Logan has told me so much about you. Now I can see where he gets his lovely blue eyes."

Oh, but that pleased his grandmother. *Nice recovery, Jen.*

"He also gets his good looks from the Parker side," his grandmother declared.

Logan refrained from pointing out that her daughter-in-law, his mother, also had blonde hair and blue eyes, and had been a *Miss Texas* finalist back in the day. Traits were a grab bag, as he'd learned from studying genetics. Although he hadn't given much thought to *his* DNA until Jen had expressed an interest.

He gestured in the direction of the fireplace, starting on the left. "My dad, Sullivan Hardt."

"Pleased to meet you." His father's frown wouldn't convince anyone that he was pleased about anything. Logan ignored his dad's perpetual bad mood and moved on.

Jake had his arms crossed over his chest and stood with his legs braced, identical to their dad, right down to the frown. Was he even aware of it?

"Next to dad is my brother, Jake. He's a sheriff's deputy, and he's the oldest—"

"You do look older than dad," Clay quipped, before he

snatched off his sweat-stained hat and made a sweeping bow. "I'm Clay. I'm *not* old, and I'm better looking."

"You've got gray in your hair," Jake pointed out.

Clay's cocky smile faltered. He ran his fingers through his shaggy hair, which *did* look like it had more white strands threaded through the sandy brown. "That's not gray. It's blond, like Logan's."

Jake ignored him. "Riding bulls ages a man. He'll be hobbling around with a cane while I'm still dancing the two-step."

Miss Kate zinged a sharp look their way—translated, *put a lid on it*—before turning back with a polite smile. "Did you take Jen by the hotel to meet Austin?" Miss Kate spoke loud enough for his dad to hear. She knew Austin wouldn't come out here, that he'd burned the bridge behind him when he'd last left home. She also knew who needed to work harder at rebuilding it.

Logan nodded. "Yes, ma'am, I did. We met for breakfast." He'd kept Jen in bed for twelve hours beforehand, but he didn't mention that.

"Why don't you bring Jen's bag in from the car. Put it upstairs, in the room across from mine."

Perhaps Miss Kate *had* figured it out. She wanted Jen where she could keep an eye on her.

The lines on her face softened as she put her hand on Jen's shoulder. "I'm sure you'd like to freshen up. Logan can show you to your room."

He gladly took the cue, eager to get Jen out of the spotlight and see if she was feeling up to eating lunch. Subjecting her to a family gathering so soon in their relationship might've been a big mistake. He didn't want to scare her off before he had a chance to get a lasso on her. He hadn't told anyone his plans—that was something the two of them would discuss first—but he got the sense his grandmother knew he'd found the right girl, because she'd been after him to bring Jen out to the ranch.

The room she'd been assigned faced the front of the

house, which overlooked the pond. She'd have a nice view. As soon as he set her suitcase down, she shut the door behind them and leaned against the wall with her eyes closed. Worry shot through him, and he took a step in case he needed to catch her. "You all right?"

"Oh my God. I can't *believe* I threw up in front of your family." She pressed her lips together like she was fighting a smile.

He released his relief with a laugh. "You have to admit, it broke the ice."

Her shoulders started shaking, and then she leaned over, holding her middle, and snorted. "Don't. Don't make me laugh. They'll hear us, and think I'm crazy *and* gross."

Logan pulled her into a reassuring embrace. "Oh, now, you weren't gross."

"I was too! Don't bother lying to me. By the way, I need to thank Huston for coming up with something even more disgusting — you throwing up in his boots."

"His *new* boots. He was so proud of them, and I was jealous because I hadn't gotten a new pair too."

"You did it on purpose?"

"No, I really was carsick, and I couldn't find anything in the back except his boots. He accused me of doing it on purpose though. After I'd puked in them, he refused to wear them, even after Dad cleaned them out."

She giggled against his chest. "That is so funny."

"I'm glad you aren't angry." He kissed her hair.

Leaning back, she gazed up at him with surprise. "Why would I be angry?"

"Because I pushed you into meeting my family. I knew you were nervous, but I didn't realize you were so scared you'd make yourself sick."

She lowered her lashes and dipped her head, and after a moment, detached herself from his arms. "I'm not angry with you."

He wanted to believe her, but there was something she wasn't telling him. Granted, he could've waited a little longer to bring her home, but he was eager for his family to get to know her before he proposed.

She opened the suitcase on the bed, removed a small organizer bag, and took out a toothbrush. "I have a bad taste in my mouth. I'll just be a minute and then we can go back down."

After she went into the adjoining bathroom, he heard the water running.

Possibly, she was upset because he'd told her she would be sleeping alone, in another house. After they finished lunch, he would show her around, including some of places they could sneak off to and get frisky. He hadn't lived here all his life without discovering—or learning from his brothers—the best spots to take girls.

Living apart had been harder than he'd imagined. Nightly phone calls, texts and emails weren't enough to satisfy him. The more he talked to her and got to know her, the more certain he was that he wanted her in his life permanently. The rest of the details were something they could work out.

By the time he and Jen made it back to the dining room, his brothers were prowling around the table. They'd waited for their guest, but they wouldn't have waited for him. Then again, if Jen weren't with him, he wouldn't be the last one to the table either. He'd learned the law of survival: Show up first and eat fast.

During lunch, Miss Kate kept up a steady conversation with Jen, while peppering in questions about Atlanta and her job in advertising. Logan munched on tacos, but kept his attention on Jen, knowing how much she hated being the center of attention. Despite her unfortunate entrance, she seemed to be handling the inquisition well enough. He'd intercede if need be.

"And your parents? Are they still living?" Miss Kate asked.

"Yes, alive and kicking, and happily leading separate lives." Jen turned to Logan. "Would you mind passing the salsa?"

"Sure." He handed over the bowl. If she had an upset stomach before, she must be over it. Or more likely she'd asked for the salsa to change the subject because she didn't like to discuss her family. His grandmother wasn't being nosy. It just wouldn't occur to her that someone wouldn't be comfortable talking about family—her favorite subject. She'd already recited the family tree while Jen pretended interest. Or maybe it wasn't pretend. Jen seemed to be into their genealogy, as well as his genetics. Fortunately, her interest in sex had gone beyond procreation, although he'd love nothing better than to have children with her, and they weren't using protection.

He wiped his hands and put his napkin on the table, then leaned back in his chair. Time to rescue his princess. "Think I'll show Jen around the ranch after lunch."

She shot a brief, grateful look his way. He'd guessed right about the salsa. "That sounds like fun. I'm interested in seeing more of the ranch, especially the horses, and that old western town. Logan told me the buildings were made from shipping containers, and you ordered vintage false fronts to make them look like old stores, and there's even a jail. I've seen people use those containers to build tiny homes. I'll bet they'd make great guest quarters."

His father's head came up—until now he hadn't been acting like he was paying attention. Jen didn't realize she'd broached a sensitive subject,. She'd just switched the conversation to something she felt comfortable discussing. Logan berated himself for not warning her when she'd been asking all those questions.

"Oh honey, I agree, we should turn those buildings into guest houses. Carly and I talked about that—she's the boys' mother. You two would've gotten along like litter pups. She was creative, too, and had lots of ideas. She even had designs drawn up. I'll show them to you..."

Miss Kate's avid interest only made things worse. She'd pushed like the devil to get his father to move ahead with his mother's crazy idea. Okay, maybe not crazy. His mom had been a starry-eyed romantic and had fallen in love on this ranch and thought everybody else would too.

Jake, Clay and Huston had stopped eating. Tense postures suggested a tornado alert, not surprising, considering the deepening frown on their dad's face, which everyone knew was a warning. Except for Miss Kate. She knew, but she wasn't a bit intimidated. She'd go toe-to-toe with an angry bull.

"Those are storage buildings," their father stated. "We don't need guest houses."

Logan frowned, his anger building. That was rude...both to Jen, and to Miss Kate.

His grandmother stiffened her backbone—as if it wasn't stiff enough. "We'll need them when we start getting more guests. There are only five extra rooms in this house."

"We *won't be* getting more guests, because we're running a ranch, not a resort." His father's declaration seemed to echo in the silent dining room. The tension in the air grew so thick it was a miracle anyone could breathe, and Jen looked like she was about the throw up again.

Logan's patience, already frayed, snapped. He reached beneath the table for Jen's hand and squeezed reassuringly, while facing his father with a set jaw. "Jen was making a suggestion. She's got the right to her opinion without you stomping on it."

His dad's gathered brows lifted in surprise. Logan knew why. He was generally the one who tried to pacify his dad and make peace. But he'd be damned if he let a sour old cowpoke get away with bullying Jen—or his grandmother, for that matter.

Jake cleared his throat. "So... Jen, you haven't told us how you two met."

The abrupt shift nearly gave Logan whiplash. Fortunately, it also jerked him out of escalating anger and saved him from calling his father out. He picked up his glass and took a sip of iced tea to cool down. He'd been ready to punch his dad in the nose.

"How we met? I, uh, I live next door to Logan's friend, Troy, and he and Celeste were planning a backyard wedding and Logan was helping get things ready..." Jen spoke fast, like she was trying to get everything out in a hurry. "He came over to trim my bushes."

Logan sucked in a sharp breath, sending tea down the wrong way. He burst out coughing.

Clay, sitting next to him, smacked him between the shoulder blades. "Must've been a doozy of a first date."

A smartass. That was all they needed.

Still coughing, Logan got up to leave the room, rather than sit there hacking. He couldn't believe Jen had dropped that bomb. What was she thinking?

She leapt up and followed him into the kitchen where she began to rub his back, which was a whole lot better than the beating Clay had given him. "Are you all right?"

He nodded. After a moment, he regained his ability to speak without coughing. "Did you do that on purpose?" he asked in a harsh whisper.

Her cheeks, which were already pink, darkened to a deeper shade. "Are you kidding? No. I was nervous, and it just slipped out. You scared me. It looked like you and your dad were about to pull out your six-shooters."

"If I called him out, I'd use my fists." At her horrified expression, he clasped her shoulder, and let her know with a smile that he was teasing. "Don't worry. I won't beat him up too badly."

The fluttering eye-roll signaled she'd regained her sense of humor, as well as her composure. "It can't get any worse..." She threw a worried glance over her shoulder. "Unless you told them about me asking you to be a donor? Maybe that explains your father's baleful glares."

"Only Huston knows. If he'd said anything, *I* would've heard about it, believe me." Needing to comfort her, or maybe he was the one who needed comfort, he reached out and gathered her hands. They were so slender, the bones light, like a bird's, making him achingly aware of how fragile she could be. At the same time, she had strength in ways he lacked. For one, her persistence in going after what she wanted, all alone, if need be. She wouldn't be alone any longer.

"What *have* you told them about me?" Her brow furrowed. He could almost see the wheels turning inside her mind. She thought he'd brought her home so his family could hand down a judgment, and she'd worried herself sick about making a good impression, because she wanted to be accepted. He wanted that too, but never doubted his family would love her once they got to know her—if only his dad wouldn't act like such an ass.

He had gone about this the wrong way. First, he should've proposed, and then brought her home as his fiancée. She would be more confident of her place in the family. More importantly, she wouldn't doubt his feelings for her. *That*, he could fix. He couldn't do a damn thing about his dad's ill temper, and refused to wear the mantle of peacemaker any longer. He had Jen to think about.

"Let's go outside." He slipped his arm around her waist. "I want to talk to you. Privately."

Chapter Twelve

From the kitchen, Jen followed Logan through the back door, which opened out onto a wrap-around porch. They descended a few steps, and then he took her hand and led her away at a fast clip. Was he anxious to get away from the tension? He might be embarrassed because of the off-color remark she'd let slip, or it was possible she'd rattled him by bringing up that western town. Good Lord, she might as well have kicked a hornet's nest into the middle of the room. She wouldn't go anywhere near *that* subject again.

Running away wasn't Logan's style, nor was it an option. She had to go back and at least try to make peace with Logan's father. Being the reason they were at odds left her with a sick feeling in her stomach that had nothing to do with pregnancy. "Won't they think it's odd that we left without saying anything?"

"Don't worry about it."

"Telling me not to worry, without telling me what's wrong, isn't helping."

"Nothing's wrong." He tightened his hold on her hand. "Trust me."

"I do trust you." She trusted him enough to step out into

uncertainty with this relationship, and to be paraded in front of his family, despite her reservations. What more did she have to do to prove her faith in him?

The road they were on led down to a large red and white building, which Logan had told housed the stables. A man, also wearing a cowboy hat, stood in the center of a corral holding a lead rope, while a horse pranced in circles around him. In a pasture were more horses of varying colors: gray, chestnut, bay, a few spotted and paint. Just seeing them, out there grazing peacefully, made her calmer.

"I love horses. I always dreamed of owning one, but my father was allergic to them and my mother was afraid. They let me take lessons, though, and I hung around the stables—until we moved again."

"You could be around horses all the time if you lived here." Logan's offhand remark surprised her. He didn't expect her to move out here, had never mentioned it. His comment was merely an observation, or he was joking, to lighten the mood. Lord knows she needed something to elevate her sagging spirits.

"I've heard of working remotely, but this is *really* remote," she quipped. "Do you even have internet?"

"Dial up."

"Very funny. No one uses dial up anymore."

"Except out here."

He was kidding. They weren't marooned on another planet.

She inhaled deeply. The air smelled fresh and clean...and with a hint of manure, but she didn't mind it. Logan obviously loved growing up out here. A child would have plenty of things to do, other than play video games or zone out on a cell phone. Why, she'd barely looked at her phone, or watch, since they'd arrived.

The noonday sun heated her head. She could understand now why everyone wore hats, and made a mental note to pick one up before she made another trip to Texas...*if* she made another trip. She'd have to pass muster with his family first, and she'd set herself back, oh, by a year or so, with that *helpful* suggestion.

"I wish you'd warned me about the western town being off limits."

Logan smiled at her with understanding. "None of that was *your* fault. My dad behaved like a donkey. He's argued for a long time with Miss Kate about the resort idea. It's not going to happen, but she can be a donkey, too. I guarantee she likes you, though. You're smart and outspoken, like my mom…and she thought my mom hung the moon."

Jen leaned against Logan's arm. How did he always know just the right thing to say when she was beating herself up? "Thank you. I didn't know your mother, but from what you've told me, I'm sure we would've hit it off. And I see what you mean about Miss Kate being tough. I like her…a lot."

Logan veered off the gravel and onto the grass, leading her toward the pond. Two canoes and a paddleboat were tied up to a dock. A mallard couple glided on the dark surface; the male sported flashy green plumage, while the female had subtle brown coloring, which allowed her to fade into the grass along the shoreline where she'd hide her ducklings. Jen's right brain came alive and imagined how she'd paint the bucolic scene.

"This is a beautiful setting."

"It was a cattle pond before my mother decided our guests would enjoy something prettier to look at. Dad moved the cows and built a dock."

For a man not committed to his wife's vision, Logan's father had done a lot to please her.

"Your father must've loved your mother very much." Jen shared her insight, not because Logan didn't know, but because he needed to hear it, and not remain angry with his father. She'd harbored bitterness against her parents for years, and all it did was make her unhappy.

Logan's expression remained pensive. "He still loves her. I don't know if he'll ever get over his grief."

Jen's heart ached for the older man's pain. She hadn't lost a spouse, or a parent, but she'd been dealing with overwhelming emotions for years. Grief didn't excuse his bad behavior, but it certainly explained it. "Sometimes people get stuck emotionally. If your dad followed through with your mother's plan, it might surprise him how good he'd feel, especially knowing how much she wanted it."

"Maybe...I don't know. But it was worth a suggestion, and I'm proud of you for trying." Logan stopped at a bench beneath a big shade tree, and after she sat down, he put his arm around her. Wanting to bring back his smile, she lifted her face for a kiss. He brushed his lips against hers in a way that seemed intended to arouse. It worked.

"You said you'd show me some *interesting* places," she murmured. "Out here on this bench isn't one of them, is it?"

"I'm game if you are," he whispered.

"Mm. I'm not really into voyeurism." She peered over his shoulder, half-expecting to see his family crowded on the front porch, watching. If they'd stay inside, she might take him up on his offer to get playful on the bench.

"What are you smiling about?"

"Was I smiling?"

"Oh yeah, big smile."

She had to stop daydreaming about making love out in the open, and living some idyllic life out in the country. As nice as it seemed in her imagination, it wouldn't work out in reality. Not now...maybe not ever, and not just because she'd messed up the family meet-and-greet. She wouldn't know what to do, or how to be useful. She didn't belong here.

If she told Logan about the baby and asked him to move to Atlanta to be with her, he might. He'd promised he wouldn't abandon them. But then he wouldn't get around to returning to school, and she wouldn't ask him to sacrifice his dreams...again. After he finished school, they could talk about where to live. "Have you reapplied to vet school? I have a check with your name on it."

Her offer was met with a frown. "I told you I don't want to be paid."

Oh good lord, they'd gone round and round about this. "Consider it a gift."

He gazed out over the pond without answering. His pride was getting in the way. Either that, or he'd decided he didn't want to go back to school, even though he'd talked like he planned to go back.

"Have you changed your mind?"

"No. I still want to finish school. I'll take out a loan."

She released a frustrated breath. "All right then, I'm offering you an *interest-free* loan. There's no good reason for you to refuse that."

He shifted on the bench, facing her. "Do you know what it costs? Over two hundred thousand by the time I graduate. Why would you loan me that much money?"

"Why?" she echoed. How could he ask her that? He had to know she'd do anything to help him. She'd all but told him she'd fallen in love with him. But he hadn't actually told her he loved *her*. He'd said he wanted to give their relationship a chance. That remark about her moving out here, possibly he meant it and was testing her.

She toyed with her watch, more uneasy than interested in looking at it. If she moved, she'd have to quit her job, and then what the hell would she do? Suggest the agency open an office in one of those little western buildings?

Besides, he hadn't outright asked her to move, and he'd given her no guarantees. She ought to be testing him. "You told me you wanted to go back to school and become a veterinarian. I want to you to do that too, and I'm willing to invest in your education. Who knows, maybe you'll decide to set up a practice in Atlanta."

He brushed back a strand of hair the breeze had blown into her face. "Is that what you want?"

Her breath caught. She started to say *yes*, she'd dreamed of him finishing school and deciding to come back to be with her. But those were dreams about a future that wasn't here yet, and his solemn expression made it clear that wasn't *his* dream. If she told him what she really wanted—to have him *and* her career—he'd see how selfish she could be and he'd run the other way. In fact, she was so selfish, she couldn't let him go even if she couldn't make him happy. Somehow, she would figure out how they could both get what they wanted.

"What I *want* is for you to go back to school. I'll come out to visit as often as possible. That's what we planned, right?" She gripped his hand and searched his eyes for affirmation. They really were as blue as the Texas sky stretched out above them. In them, she saw reflected the tenderness that was so much a part of him, and something else; something that squeezed her heart and made her regret not giving him what he'd indirectly asked for, and deserved—her complete and total devotion.

"Logan, I…" She tried to find the courage to tell him she was sorry she wasn't as strong as him. She didn't know how to care as deeply as he did.

Before she could say anything more, he covered her mouth and gave her a deep, deep kiss. One that stole every fear and doubt she'd ever had. With a kiss, he drank in what she couldn't find the strength to give him. He continued kissing her until she clung to him and her resistance melted.

He ended the kiss and rested his forehead against hers, slipping his hand around the back of her neck. "I love you, Jen" he said a rough voice. "I want to be with you, no matter what. Tell me what *you* want."

Overcome, she could only lift her hand to his cheek to stroke his face. Her chest ached, hearing him say words that only confirmed what she'd at last come to realize, what he'd shown her, time and again, but she hadn't recognized it, because she'd never before experienced the kind of unconditional love he offered her.

"I want you to be happy," she whispered. Those were the truest words she'd ever spoken. Of all men, Logan deserved happiness, and she wanted to give it to him. Instinctively, she knew there was one thing she could give him right now that would bring him joy. She brought his hand to her stomach and held it against the spot where a new life formed. "Logan, I'm carrying your baby."

Amazement dawned in his eyes, then moisture formed along his lower lids. Seeing his tears triggered her own.

"A baby," he said in a hushed voice. "*Our* baby." With a whoop, he grabbed her, and started hugging and kissing her. "Jen, that's wonderful…it's…it's…"

He pulled back with a look of sudden awareness. "That's why you got sick."

She nodded, wiping away tears with the back of her hand. "I think so. Or it might've been nerves. I haven't gotten sick before today."

"Do we need to go back to Fort Worth? Find a doctor?"

"I have a doctor's appointment next week to make sure everything is all right. But I feel good, really good." She gathered his hands and kissed his knuckles. "I think what we need to do is make plans. About our future."

Whatever she had to do to keep this wonderful man by her side, she'd do it, even if he asked her to move to the moon—or to the middle of Texas. Who knew how long they might have. Neither of them had any guarantees. His father and mother hadn't known they would be parted early, yet all she had to do was look around to know they'd made the most of their time together. In the end, nothing else mattered except the life she and Logan created. Together.

Jen circled her arms around his neck. "I love you, Logan. I'll do whatever it takes for us to stay together."

He cradled her face with his big hands and gave her the sweetest, most tender kiss. For such a big, strong man, he could be so gentle. "So will I."

Her heart thrilled to his promise.

Over his shoulder, something caught her eye, a movement. The deputy, Logan's oldest brother, Jake, got into his patrol car, and a moment later, the dust flew as he roared down the gravel drive.

"Looks like your brother got tired of waiting."

Logan paused from nibbling on her ear. "Jake isn't known for patience. But he was on his lunch break, so he had to get back to work."

She felt bad for leaving so abruptly, and after his brothers had made a special effort to be here to meet her. They'd been welcoming and funny, and had tried to make her feel comfortable, and so had Miss Kate. Jen suspected Logan's dad might regret what had happened. Anyone who loved his wife as much as he did could be forgiven for letting grief get the best of him. Somehow, she would win him over, and she would also carve out her own place in this family, because they would become her family too.

"Do you think we should go back to the house?"

"Not yet." Logan kissed the end of her nose and his smile turned mischievous. "I still want to show you one of those *interesting* places…"

Chapter Thirteen

College Station, Texas, three months later

Logan pulled the door to the bedroom closed, slowly releasing the knob to avoid making noise. He'd hoped to be home before ten, but he'd been cramming for an exam, and then had gotten a call to assist one of the vets with an emergency. Being a first-year DVM student, he'd been fortunate to land a job at a local clinic, and knew better than to say no when they asked for help.

He made his way to the bathroom, brushed his teeth in the dark, then groped his way to the closet where he undressed down to his briefs. So far so good...

The mattress sank as he crawled into bed and slipped under the covers.

"Mm." Jen rolled over and reached across him, at the same time drawing her knee to his hip. Her soft lips touched his and her bare breasts brushed against his chest, giving him a jolt.

"Hi, cowboy," she murmured.

"Hey, baby." He kissed her, smoothing his hand along her bare side. "You're naked."

"I even took off my watch."

"No watch? You know how that turns me on." He reached up and slid his fingers through her silky hair, cradling her head to bring her to him for another kiss, this one deeper and lasting long enough to make him hard. "I'm surprised you're still awake."

"I wasn't. I woke up when you got into bed."

"Sorry 'bout that."

"Don't be sorry. I intended to wait for you, but I get tired earlier these days."

"You're up now?" He hoped the answer would be *yes*.

She put her lips to his ear, giving him goose bumps when she released a soft laugh. "I think you are. Up, I mean." Her fingers glided over the front of his briefs where his arousal strained.

He caught a sharp breath, and released it on a groan.

"Mm, I've missed you too," she murmured. "Let's get reacquainted."

He couldn't get his britches off fast enough.

Moments later, he sank into her welcoming arms. Just when he thought making love with Jen couldn't get any better, it did. The aftermath was just as sweet. Entwined, they kissed and stroked each other's cooling bodies.

For three more months that had seemed like forever, they'd maintained a long-distance relationship. On weekends, she usually flew to Texas, into Houston, close enough for him to pick her up at the airport and bring her back to where he attended school.

Jen had insisted he follow through with his plans to go back to A&M and finish his doctorate in veterinary medicine. She knew him so well. Without her persistent encouragement, he might've stayed on the ranch out of obligation. That wouldn't have made him happy, and eventually, he would've come to resent the very people he loved enough to give up his dreams. Jen wouldn't let him. She'd even set up a fund to help him financially, after he'd swallowed his pride and accepted her generous offer. He'd promised he would pay her back. She told him he already had.

He slid his hand over the slight swell of her abdomen. She'd given him a hell of a lot more than financial support. She'd given him hope that he would have what he wanted most—a life with Jen and their baby.

"Are you here all weekend?"

"I'm here for as long as you want me to be."

Logan drew back. Damn, he wished he could see her face so he'd know if she was joking. "What if I say I want you here forever?"

"I'm not sure this apartment will be big enough for the three of us *forever*." Her voice held a hint of amusement.

His heart thudded harder. She had promised they would stay together and he believed her. Working that out hadn't happened overnight, but he refused to rush her. "Are you joking?"

"Why would I joke about that? I told you I want us to be together. I've taken a different job so I can work remotely."

Work *remotely?* Houston wasn't the end of the universe. Or did she mean...? When they'd visited the ranch, she'd seemed to enjoy it, yet appeared reluctant to consider the possibility of living there one day. At one time, he had planned to move back and open a large animal practice close by. But then he'd fallen in love with Jen, and his plans had become secondary to their mutual happiness.

"Remotely? As in anywhere?"

"I was thinking about how nice it would be to raise our children on a ranch."

He wanted to leap up, jump on the bed, and yodel with glee, yet he managed to restrain himself. He didn't want her to feel pressured into it, just because she knew that was his dream. She'd told him she wanted him to be happy. He wanted her to be happy too.

He pressed a kiss on her hair, which smelled fresh and clean and faintly of vanilla. "You love that job, and your home, and being in Atlanta. Are you sure you want to leave it all behind?"

She cuddled closer and nuzzled his neck. "Mm, I do like Atlanta and my job, but I *love* you. And I think I could get used to living on a ranch, if you promise we can have our own house...with indoor plumbing...and Wi-Fi, not dial-up."

"Absolutely. I know just the place to build. Private, *interesting...*" He drew her to him for a kiss, and she returned his kiss with so much passion, it took his breath away.

In between kisses, she whispered, "Let's get married at the ranch before the baby's born."

He thought he couldn't be happier? He grinned and moved his hands down to her waist, still amazed by the miracle of her carrying his child, and loving him enough to make a new life with him. "Did you just propose to me?"

"Should I get down on one knee?"

"I can think of a better position."

"Like this?" She moved over, straddling him, then leaned down and began to nuzzle his neck. Feeling her touch and the press of her body, without being able to see much, heightened the erotic sensation. He lay back and held the reins on his eagerness while she explored him with her lips and hands.

"I will," he gasped.

"Will what?"

"Marry you."

"Good. Our baby deserves two parents who'll always be there for each other...and for him."

Logan snapped his eyes open. *Him?* Was that a convenient term, or had she meant to say it? Jen was precise, exact. She always used "him or her"—both, not just one or the other.

A sense of wonder washed over him. "It's a boy?"

"It's a boy," she murmured in his ear. "And I hope he

has blue eyes and blond hair and grows up to look just like his daddy."

Logan's heart swelled so full, it filled his chest. If he got all serious and mushy, he'd soon be bawling like a baby. "You better be glad it's boy. A girl wouldn't appreciate having size fifteen feet."

Jen sat back. "Size *fifteen?*" She put her hand to her mouth. In the darkness, he could make out her form, but not the expression on her face.

"Are you sick?"

"No—" She started laughing. "No wonder you're so...so..."

Logan grabbed her arms and rolled her over, taking care not to crush her beneath his weight. Yeah, he was big. Everywhere. "I'm so good at satisfying you. That's what you mean."

She looped her arms around his neck and shifted to allow him to fit into the cradle of her hips. "Yes, you *are* good at that, cowboy. I don't think I could be more satisfied."

"Allow me to prove you wrong, ma'am."

The story of the *Texas Hardts* continues...
Watch for the next installment, *A Cowboy's Promise*,
coming out Fall 2017

From the Author

I hope you enjoyed *Maybe Baby*, which kicks off a new Contemporary Romance series, *Texas Hardts*. I loved writing Jen and Logan's romance. You'll see them again in the next novel in the new series, along with Logan's brothers. The Hardts are descendants of Ross Hardt, a major character in my historical romance series, *The Bride Train*. You can learn more about Ross in his story, *Seducing Susannah, Book 4, The Bride Train Series*

Find an up-to-date listing of other titles on my website under My Books. Also, please consider posting a short review. Honest reader reviews help others decide if they'll enjoy a book.

Be among the first to know when I have a new release when you sign up for my email newsletter. As a new subscriber you'll receive a free book just for signing up.

You can connect with me on Facebook, Twitter and Pinterest, or send me an email (eeburke@eeburke.com). I love to hear from readers!

Warmest Regards,
E.E. Burke

Books by E.E. Burke

Texas Hardts Series
Contemporary Romance
MAYBE BABY

The Bride Train Series
Historical Romance
VALENTINE'S ROSE
PATRICK'S CHARM
TEMPTING PRUDENCE
SEDUCING SUSANNAH

American Mail-Order Brides
Historical Romance
VICTORIA BRIDE OF KANSAS
SANTA'S MAIL-ORDER BRIDE

Steam! Romance and Rails Series
Historical Romance
HER BODYGUARD
KATE'S OUTLAW
A DANGEROUS PASSION
FUGITIVE HEARTS

Audiobooks by E.E. Burke
VICTORIA, BRIDE OF KANSAS
SANTA'S MAIL ORDER BRIDE

www.eeburke.com

To learn about upcoming and new releases,
please join my newsletter:

https://www.eeburke.com/news.html

Warm, witty…a little wild. That's what you'll find when you pick up a book by bestselling author E.E. Burke. Her chosen setting is the American West, and her latest series, *The Bride Train*, features a cast of unusual characters thrown together through a misguided bride lottery. *Maybe Baby* is her first Contemporary Romance, and features…who else, but a handsome modern-day cowboy!

Other series include *Steam! Romance and Rails*, which follows the lives of dangerous men and daring women caught up in a cutthroat competition as the railroads advance across the frontier. Her novella, *Victoria, Bride of Kansas*, part of the unprecedented *American Mail-Order Brides* series, is a Kindle Top 100 Bestseller and a semifinalist in the 2016 Kindle Best Book Awards.

E.E., also known as Elisabeth, has earned accolades in regional and national contests, including the RWA's prestigious Golden Heart®. Over the years, she's been a disc jockey, a journalist and an advertising executive, before finally getting around to living the dream—writing stories readers can get lost in.

www.ingramcontent.com/pod-product-compliance
Lightning Source LLC
Chambersburg PA
CBHW070926130626
46555CB00001B/310